Late for Square Dancing

By

M K Scott

Books by M K Scott

The Talking Dog Detective Agency
Cozy Mystery
A Bark in the Night
Requiem for a Rescue Dog Queen
Bark Twice for Danger
The Ghostly Howl
Dog Park Romeo

The Painted Lady Inn Mysteries Series
Culinary Cozy Mystery
Murder Mansion
Drop Dead Handsome
Killer Review
Christmas Calamity
Death Pledges a Sorority
Caribbean Catastrophe
Weddings Can be Murder
The Skeleton Wore Diamonds
Death of a Honeymoon
Cakewalk to Murder
Sailors Take Warning (Spring 2020)

The Way Over the Hill Gang Series
Cozy Mystery
Late for Dinner
Late for Bingo
Late for Shuffleboard
Late for Square Dancing

Chapter One

E VEN THOUGH THE trees had cast off their autumn finery, the sun still shone bright and there wasn't even a hint of approaching winter in the air. The unexpected warm stretch had lured people outside with mothers pushing strollers and kids riding bikes. Even a few folks were out cutting grass. At the head of the neighborhood where Greener Pastures Convalescent Center stood, the parking lot was full, but the only person spotted outside was a nurse's aide half-hidden in the building's shadow, furtively smoking a cigarette next to the no smoking sign.

Loud music poured from the doorway another employee pushed open as she left. There was a shout of *do-si-do!* before the door swung shut. The departing employee waved at the smoker, then headed for her car at a jog as if eager to leave. Inside the center, however, the pace of the day differed.

The sounds of clicking, music, and a man who occasionally called out random commands, such as bow to your corner or bow to your partner, filled the corridors surrounding the large dining room. Inside the room, residents were crowded so closely together that it wouldn't be a surprise if their wheelchair wheels got entangled.

At a table closest to the door, three people sat: a short, bald man, and two women. The first had her blonde hair arranged in an elaborate style and lacquered into place by a liberal dose of hair spray. She winced a little but had her head tilted in the direction of a wiry woman whose lips were moving.

"This is how it works, Lola," the woman explained while gesturing to the dancers. "The man calls out the moves for the dancers, then they have to do what he tells them to do."

"Eunice," Lola sighed and managed an eye roll at the same time, "I know how square-dancing works. This isn't my first encounter, you know."

"Ha!" Eunice tossed her head, bouncing her gray-threaded curls. "I figured that being a former Vegas showgirl, your extent of dancing involved teetering around on high heels, waving feather fans."

The man sitting with them coughed, earning a sympathetic glance from Lola. "You okay, Gus? Need some water?"

He met her gaze, then shook his head as he pushed up to standing. "Think I'll go back to my room and get some water."

Both women watched Gus leave, then Eunice leaned closer to say, "He has no clue what you said. He's already hard of hearing, but with…" She gestured to a nearby speaker. "…the music blasting, he doesn't hear a word."

While the music may have a few residents tapping their toes, it did nothing for those who *could* hear. Lola pursed her lips and wrinkled her nose before speaking. "You'd think they're trying to deafen the rest of us. I'm leaving, too." Lola reached for her walker and stood. She glanced back over her shoulder to address Eunice's earlier comment. "Showgirl routines are choreographed. Some of it is quite complicated. We certainly never needed someone yelling instructions on a microphone."

Eunice gave a derisive sniff. Even though both she and Lola were part of Senior Sleuths, a covert group within the center that solved cold cases, it was still fun to poke at the woman. After all, what woman wouldn't feel a little uncomfortable around a former showgirl. Getting the aged blonde riled up evened the playing field, especially considering Eunice's skinny form and acerbic nature didn't make her popular with the opposite gender. Thank goodness for Gus, who had been waiting for a forceful woman to take charge of him.

Making friends was not something Eunice did easily. Her father once told her she should laugh at the other children's jokes and occasionally compliment them on something they did. He also told her to be honest at all times. Talk about a paradox. It was hard to be honest and popular. Eventually, she settled on being honest and helpful, even when the help wasn't wanted. Was it too late to change her ways? Better yet, did she want to?

One of the lady dancers, whose colorful skirt stood out with its multitude of petticoats, interrupted Eunice's reflections and invited her to join in. Someone had deliberately picked her. Woo hoo! She jumped up and tried to ignore that most of the other attendees were in wheelchairs. That had nothing to do with them picking her. Obviously, the dancer recognized in Eunice a born square dancer.

The dancer had a firm grip on Eunice's arm as if afraid she might fall and guided her through the steps. Opposite of them were a few other residents being herded in a similar manner. Such behavior might be expected for one of the more confused residents, but Eunice didn't need that type of treatment and shook off her helping hand. "I can follow directions," she shouted to her helper, who smiled back with an apologetic grin.

3

By keeping an eye on the dancer in front of her, Eunice mimicked the moves, albeit a few seconds late, which made her a little bit out of step. Of course, if she knew what the commands meant, she'd be golden. If the home had lessons, instead of randomly bringing in a group to demonstrate, then she'd be all over it. That was the problem with the center's activities director. She trotted people in to demonstrate, assuming that everyone was so old they'd never want to do something on their own.

The previous shuffleboard tournament had been a result of constant complaining about endless bingo, which had been the sum of their activities. One tournament, while fun, did not change the daily bingo games. The rumor was the occasional church handbell choir or scout troop that showed up came by choice and were not solicited by the director. Even this group was associated with the receptionist, who stood on the sidelines, clapping. Eunice blinked when she noticed the dancers had formed two lines, leaving her stranded in the middle. It must be a dance circle. Time to be the spotlight dancer. She placed her hands on her hips and placed one foot out while trying to recall the tap lessons she had taken as a kid. Nothing was coming. The original dancer who had invited her to dance was waving wildly at her, then pointing to the line.

Ah, it might not be a dance circle. Just as well, since no moves had filtered back into her mind over the years. The sizable bulk of Herman, another Senior Sleuth, filled the doorway. He, too, was waving, but not necessarily in the panicky way of the dancer. He must be trying to rescue her, bless him.

She gave the line of dancers and the seated residents a hand wave worthy of the queen. "Pressing business. I must go. Carry on."

A few curious looks, muttered comments, and a lone laugh followed Eunice as she weaved her way through the people. Even though she was tempted to swing around to see who might be laughing at her, she didn't. She kept her head high and her back straight and moved toward the door.

Herman urged her out of the main room, away from the speakers. Music filtered into the hallway but faded as they strolled away from the dining room and turned into one of the adjoining corridors before trying to speak. Finally, Eunice nudged Herman with her elbow and asked, "What's up?"

Herman reached up to stroke his handlebar mustache, which was his newest affectation, and replied, "Lance is here. Marci told me to round up the sleuths."

While it might not have sounded like much to anyone who cared to eavesdrop, it pretty much summed up the situation. Marci was a detective who had been severely injured in the line of duty. A car crash that shattered her leg, along with being shot more than once, had placed her in the home, fighting to recover simple acts, such as walking. While her body was recuperating, her old partner brought her cold cases to solve. In an act of compassion, she had invited select residents to help her solve the cases. Her rationale was that some of the cases were old, and locals would know the politics and streets of days gone by.

Eunice had not been invited to join, but she was as sharp as any of them. After all, she knew they were sneaking out. It wasn't all that hard to miss Gus's bald pate or his tendency to shout everything since his hearing was impaired due to being an explosives specialist in the army. Some might call it underhanded, but she basically blackmailed her way into the group. They needed her but hadn't recognized it yet.

"Ah, a new case. About time." She rubbed her hands together. "We could use something to liven up this place."

Chapter Two

T HE OVERPOWERING SCENT of cherry deodorizer hit Herman and Eunice as they made the turn into Marci's corridor. Those on this wing could take care of themselves and were ignored by the nursing staff unless they pushed the help button inside their room.

Herman waved a hand in front of his face while Eunice coughed and complained. "Phew! There are so many other scents they could have used that would smell better."

The management of the center had changed hands, and the new team did try to make it more homelike with live plants, landscape paintings on the soft blue walls, and had even bent the rules enough to allow a resident cat. Mr. Whiskers, although beloved, made himself scarce. It might have been better to have a friendlier feline.

Herman grunted a reply to her scent comment, then headed in the direction of the slightly open door from which voices were coming. As they drew closer, Eunice strained her ears to catch the conversation. Most of the good information she got was from eavesdropping. People tended to clam up when she made an appearance.

"Lance, thank you so much for bringing Bear," Lola gushed.

The tiny dog Herman and Lola rescued from the shelter was here. Lance had agreed to take care of it as well as another dog from their last case. He often brought the dog with him when he came.

Eunice charged in front of Herman, eager to get her chance to snuggle the pooch. "Let me see that adorable ball of fur."

Lola raised an imperious eyebrow and hugged the dog closer. "I'm not finished."

"You'll never be finished," Eunice growled the words. It would be just like the woman to deny her just because she had made the comment about showgirls. If she had known Bear would be here, she might have restrained herself.

A throat clearing stopped her from glaring at Lola. A slight turn of her head revealed Lance standing at the head of the small table they were gathered around. Marci was seated off to the side as if she was backing up whatever her former partner might say.

The slightly pudgy detective resembled a good-natured school teacher or an accountant, not someone who dealt with violence and death daily. His kind eyes surveyed the group, making eye contact with each one. "As you know, I usually show up with a cold case for all of you to solve. I want to commend you on your excellent work. Today, I have an entirely different scenario and one neither Marci nor I can pursue."

While Eunice liked to pride herself on how much she helped, both Marci and Lance did the lion's share of the work by use of their contacts. Technically, this was Marci's gig, which brought up the question of why would they be bowing out. She asked, "Are you two intimidated by our unorthodox methods or is it the steel trap minds?"

Jake, the fifth member of their group, laughed. The nerve of the man. Sure, it would be fine if he laughed at himself or any of the others, but not her. His shoe polish black hair wasn't fooling anyone.

Before she could say anything, Lance continued. "I've been approached by my neighbor, who has asked for my help."

He glanced back at Marci, who smiled at him. A budding romance had sprung up between the two, and judging by the looks exchanged, it may have blossomed. Lance continued. "Anyhow, my neighbor came to me because a while back his wife left him, or so we thought. She vanished along with the car and the contents of their checking account. Even though Robert filed a missing person report, nothing came of it. It looked like a clear case of the wife, Loretta, deciding to set out on her own. Most people would go for a divorce, but others just vanish. It's easier that way."

It didn't sound like a case, which made Eunice wonder why there would be a need for an investigation. "It doesn't sound like there's anything to do."

A yip drew everyone's attention to Bear, and there were a few *ahs* as they grinned at the furry bundle Lola passed to Gus. *Wait a minute.* Lola knew Eunice wanted her dog time and had just ignored her. Thankfully, Gus passed the dog to her. "Thanks, sweetie."

Lance held up one finger and cleared his throat. "Good point Eunice."

She beamed. The man might not be tall, dark, and handsome, but he did have good manners. She nodded for him to continue.

"Anyhow," Lance dropped his hand as he spoke, "a letter finally made its way to the police. It had been mailed months ago but ended up in the dead letter area due to the wrong zip code or something like that. Apparently, they're remodeling the post office and came across it. *Urgent* was written across it in red ink."

Jake steepled his fingers together in what he probably thought made him look bookish and, in turn, smart. "What did it say?"

"Basically, it was the usual thing about if anything happens to me, my husband did it."

"Hmm," Jake stroked his chin. "Did he?"

"The police have to investigate. My gut tells me no. I think no one is more baffled by the letter than Robert. This is the type of guy who stops his car and moves turtles to the other side of the road so they won't get hit. My guess is Loretta thought he might come after her since she took off with all the money, and the letter was to slow him down since the police would be investigating. Loretta never reappeared. Because of that, it gives some credence to her husband possibly killing her. The simplest solution is to find Loretta. This isn't my case, so I can't be running interference. However, if you guys found Loretta, I could pass the information along."

It didn't sound like much of a case to her. Eunice continued to pet Bear and ignored Herman who pantomimed it was his turn with the dog. "Why would we be able to find her when the police couldn't? She might be in Paris by now."

Marci chose to break in at this point. She nodded her dark head in acknowledgment. "That might seem like the case. From what Lance told me there wasn't all that much money in the account. Loretta has family and friends in the area who would hide her. She might want to enjoy the chaos she created. The woman has been waiting for the letter to come to light and considers this letter is her masterpiece. Her final jab at her husband. I'm certain even if she was in the next state, she'd show up for the show. On the other hand, this will probably be your least violent case."

The way Marci explained it, there should be very little bother. Eunice snuggled Bear under her chin as she replied. "Sounds rather boring. I'm sure I could solve it in a day with a good Internet connection."

"You?" Jake queried in a testy tone.

"If you improve your attitude, I might let you help," Eunice promised. She'd need his help since he *did* have a laptop and an Internet connection. Herman did, too, but he was under Lola's paw. No reason to say so, though.

Hands clapping silenced the murmuring that had started. Lance gestured to the group. "We will need *all* of you to work together. Maybe you missed the part about the police not finding Loretta. At the time, she probably worked extra hard to remain hidden. It could be she has become overconfident. She's probably changed her name and possibly her hair color. I have photos."

Marci passed over a manila folder from which he drew photos of a middle-aged woman carrying some weight with short hair and a fiendish gleam in her eyes. Each sleuth took a photo and considered it.

That look in Loretta's eye had Eunice turning the photo so Bear wouldn't see it. "Ah, she looks intriguing."

Intriguing wasn't the right word. *Dangerous* would have fit. To most people, she'd be just another corn-fed Midwesterner, but the gleam said otherwise to Eunice. There was a woman worthy of her snooping expertise.

Chapter Three

M ATURE TREES SHIELDED the ranch-style homes that could have existed anywhere from the 1960s on. Most had their shutters painted a shiny white, while a few opted for color. A couple of shutters even hung crooked as if a storm wind had unsettled them and the occupant had never bothered to exert any effort to fix them. Pots of yellow or orange mums near the porch enlivened a few residences. While one house had a haybale with mums grouped on it along with pumpkins, another house had clever seasonal decorations that carried through to December with a scarecrow and a Santa sharing a bench.

The five of them decided to canvas the neighborhood, possibly talk to the neighbors, and see what they could see. Eunice elbowed Gus, who was sandwiched in next to her. The man grumbled the entire trip about how Lola had stolen his shotgun position. It didn't make any difference to Gus that Herman and Lola were keeping company. He felt as a navigator he needed to be sitting up front. It wasn't as if anyone had assigned him the position. He picked up the mantle himself and often shouted directions that Herman usually ignored. In the beginning, the non-local may have listened, but he was beginning to know his way around. Besides, they all tended to give directions, and most of the time they didn't agree.

A breeze slipped into the car as Jake put down the window and inhaled audibly. "Smell that. Fall. I love autumn. Football games, apple picking, bonfires, hayrides. What's not to love?"

Every now and then, Eunice felt it was her job to bring folks back down to Earth. "Jake, you know you can't do any of that stuff. It's not like Greener Pastures will have a hayride."

Instead of being upset, he shrugged his shoulders. "Why not?" Jake arched his eyebrows and smirked. "I'm betting the center never told us we could solve cold cases, either."

He had a point. The senior sleuths operated on the premise that it was easier to ask for forgiveness as opposed to permission. So far, they hadn't had to ask for either.

Gus slapped his leg and announced, "We can have a hoedown!"

"A what?" Half the time, Gus made odd comments since his impaired hearing made it difficult to follow conversations. Even though his insurance would pay for a hearing aid, he refused to get one because that would mean he was old, resulting in replies that sometimes only made sense to Gus.

"You know, a barn dance. There could be a bonfire and bobbing for apples. Even a hayride. I've never been a fan since hay just makes me itch." He gave his head a slow shake, then peered forward at Jake with a sad expression. "Not sure how football would figure into the whole thing."

Somehow, he had heard everything Jake had said, which gave Eunice pause. Many times, she'd asked if he'd like to accompany her to the activity room for the weekly crossword tournament, and he'd answered with something like, "Cross the world? Not today." It could be the man was playing her. Eunice rejected the idea as soon as it came. That would mean he was slyer than she was, which couldn't be true. It must be Jake's deeper voice.

The car slowed, then pulled into the driveway of a neat home with red shutters but no mums. Before they left the center, Lance mentioned they could park in front of his house. Because Lance and Marci weren't on the case due to conflict of interest, they hadn't ridden along. Just as well, it was already tight enough. Still, parking in Lance's driveway wouldn't work, either. The hum of a lawnmower, along with the barking of a dog, drifted through the open window as Eunice tapped Herman's shoulder. "This won't work. No stranger parks in someone's driveway."

"Not sure if Lance wants our trooping through the neighborhood to be associated with him anyhow."

A cough, then a throat clearing, and finally Lola twisted in her seat to glare as she spoke. "Kindly keep your paws off my boyfriend. Stop telling him what to do."

No one had to tell Eunice twice. No telling what devious tricks those former showgirls had up their sleeves. Well, make that feathers, since showgirls weren't known for having sleeves. Still, Herman did not need to have his huge highway yacht parked in the good detective's driveway. People would be bound to notice, especially when the five of them popped out of the car as if they were in a clown car at the circus. Someone could be peeking through their blinds, counting and speculating at how many old folks could fit in one luxury sedan. Her lips pressed together as she contemplated other ways of making her point.

"Herman, sweetheart," Lola trilled, "I think it would be better to park on the public street. It's legal for anyone to park there. Driveways could be considered trespassing. We don't want any *nosy...*" She paused to shoot Eunice a look. "...female calling the police and all."

"You're right," Herman agreed and reversed the vehicle.

Dagnabit. Lola succeeded where Eunice had failed. It was to be expected. Men tended to pay attention to showgirls, even really old ones. The mystique, the makeup, and half a bottle of perfume played a part, too. The car lurched a little, rocking the occupants and possibly giving the appearance of a carnival ride as they jerked forward, then back. Too much more and she might need an appointment with the center's chiropractor.

"We've arrived," Herman needlessly announced. A visual inspection would have netted the same information. "Does everybody know their part?"

Who had gone and made him boss? Eunice's arms crossed on their own. Gus and she were supposed to be inviting the neighbors to church while digging into the juicy details of who might *need* to go to church. Before they left, there was a big discussion over should they be representing an actual church or a made-up one. They eventually decided on a storefront startup they'd named Mighty Precious Holy Redeemer Church. Her eighth grade English teacher would roll over in her grave with her stringing all those adjectives together. In the end, if someone actually wanted to follow their confusing directions, it would probably send them to the local auto parts store or a vacant lot.

The good news was she managed to not get the job of selling cosmetics, which had fallen to Lola this time. Herman was the confused driver looking for Eurton Avenue, while Jake reprised his role of a despairing newspaper salesman. With any luck, most would talk to the handsome, older man, but wouldn't subscribe to the paper.

Herman swing open his car door. "Ready?"

There he went again, acting like he was in charge just because he drove. If the senior sleuths had an actual leader, it would have to be Marci, who stayed behind. Just like a man to make a power grab. Eunice opened her pocketbook and pulled out a handful of pamphlets and waved them. The ones on top were actual religious tracts she'd picked up in the activity room. Most of the pile were those subscription cards that fell out of magazines with the bottom one being a perfume sample. This meant she couldn't give out her tracts willy-nilly to everyone.

"I'm ready." She gave an emphatic nod that most probably missed. "We'll have to trickle out and head different directions so it doesn't look like we're together."

Any neighborhood busybody—like the woman across the street who was kneeling beside her potted plants but was watching them with narrowed eyes—would know they came together. The best deal would be to hit her first and deflect attention. Eunice put up her hand and waved.

"Gus and I will go first. The rest of you wait five minutes, then leave. We should meet back here in an hour."

Take that, Herman! She'd grab the leadership reins back again. Since Gus was between her and the door, she stared at the door, waiting for him to open it, step out, and help her out. Underneath her breath, Eunice counted to ten and gave her sweetie a poke to move him along. He grunted, shot her a confused look, did open the door, but forgot to offer his hand. No matter. Eunice scrambled out and hooked her arm into his, then unhooked it, considering it might appear too friendly for street missionaries.

A quick survey of the street revealed a man cutting grass, a small dog sitting near the sidewalk—possibly contained by an invisible fence—and a small child riding a bicycle in a driveway. They were the kinds of things that might distract Gus. When he owned his home, he took pride in his yard and might want to give helpful advice on cutting grass. As for the dog, he was a sucker for a canine. Gus had kids and grandkids, which might make him think it was okay to talk to the young bicyclist, which could result in the mother calling 911, certain a pedophile was in the vicinity. The last possibility had her grabbing Gus's hand tightly as she moved across the street, towing him behind. Her goal was the curious woman deadheading the mums.

"Good morning!" she sang out. "How are you on this glorious Lord's day?"

The woman's suspicious expression relaxed a little as she pushed up into a standing position, grasping a trowel in her left hand. "Good. How about you?"

"Gl...," she started, then stopped, aware she'd already used the word *glorious*, but it had to be another G word, so as to not look strange. "Grand. I'm grand. How could I not be?" She added a wide toothy grin. "The sun is shining. I'm alive. What more can I ask for?"

"True," the woman agreed and crossed her arms, allowing the trowel to dangle. "That's why I'm working in the yard. The good weather won't last forever."

Eunice nodded her head, trying to decide how she'd work the needed questions into casual conversation. "You're so right, sister."

LATE FOR SQUARE DANCING

She tacked on the last because when she was a kid her family attended a Pentecostal church where everyone referred to each other as *brother* and *sister*. "My name's Eunice, and this is Brother Gus. We're here to tell you about the Precious and Cute Holy Redeemer church."

Oops. She messed up the name. There was a good chance the woman didn't notice.

"Excuse me." The resident held up her hand. "Did you say, cute?"

She had, and there wasn't an appropriate word that sounded like it. Improvise, she mentally coached herself. In a moment of absolute brilliance, she dropped Gus's arm to slap her palms together. "I did say cute? Oh, my goodness! It *is* an adorable church, I must admit. Cute is not part of its name. My mistake. I guess I start thinking about the church and cute slipped in. Anyhow, we were visiting the various neighborhoods and informing the unchurched that there is a church perfect for them."

"A noble action." The woman stated with a nod. "I have my own church, and I've been there for the last forty years."

This was the reaction Eunice had hoped for, which allowed her to execute part two of her plan. "Could you recommend any neighbor who might need the solace of a caring faith community?"

A pause ensued while the neighbor tapped her cheek and gave the matter serious thought. A mother called her child in for lunch, and the little dog went inside, too. It must be lunchtime for everyone.

"I know!" The woman exclaimed with a triumphant gleam in her eye. "There's a new couple up the street." She pointed to a house that showed signs of neglect. "They haven't been here long." She lowered her voice, making it hard to hear her as she continued speaking. "The husband even cuts the grass on *Sunday* morning."

Eunice sucked in her lips, trying to look suitably shocked at the revelation. Before she could say anything, Gus blurted out. "What about the man who killed his wife?"

"Who are you talking about?" The woman swiveled her head side to side, possibly gauging how close everyone was, then shuffled closer.

"You know..." Gus continued in a quieter tone.

Aware that he may have just stuck his foot into it, the only thing Eunice could do was try to smooth it over. "Ah, Brother Gus sometimes gets confused. We heard talk about someone going missing from around here. Too many of those television dramas have him seeing crimes where none were committed." She reached for Gus's hand and gave it a pat.

"I know who you mean," the woman volunteered. She placed one finger to her lips as her eyes rolled upward. "Her name was Leslie, Lori, something starting with an L. Colorful character. I heard she was from Puerto Rico or something. Millie, who lived close to them, said the woman was always yelling about something. She conducted most of her conversations at the top of her voice. If the husband ever said anything back, you never heard it. Fairly nice man. He still lives here, but one day the woman vanished."

"Just like that?" Eunice prompted. "Did Millie see her drive away?"

"I never asked. I didn't care for the woman. Too loud for my tastes. My only hope was she wouldn't come back."

Well, that was a fat lot of nothing. Eunice tried to compose her face into a pleasant countenance but was unsure she succeeded. She'd almost bet this woman knocked off Loretta for upsetting the dynamics of the neighborhood. "It's been good talking to you...?" She waited hopefully for a name.

"Beal, Hazel."

Bingo. Eunice managed an airy wave and steered Gus to the next house while hoping no one was there. It would be peculiar leaving after talking to only one neighbor about the impossibly cute church they were representing. They'd have to make it to the new neighbors, too, as long as Hazel was working in her yard.

Chapter Four

A SCREEN DOOR slammed and the pint-sized bike rider was back after a quick lunch. Gus and Eunice made their way down the street, discussing which house to go to next. Ideally, they wanted someplace where no one was home, which was difficult. By the look of the older sedans in the driveway, it looked as if many were home and possibly retired, too. As an older person, Eunice was well aware many liked to talk, mostly about their grandchildren and in some cases, their great-grandchildren.

When it looked like Gus might try to talk to the bike rider, she steered him across the street to a house with no car in the drive. It didn't guarantee that no one was there since people could easily park inside the garage, but she was hopeful.

"Here!" she hissed the words.

Gus kept moving down the street, unaware she had said anything. *Figures.* Her eyes narrowed as she contemplated if he heard her or not. In their short acquaintance, she noticed his hearing tended to come and go. When something mattered to him, such as a football game, he usually heard it. It could be because he saw the game and the information was printed on the screen, but he never asked what was said. Letting go of his arm once they crossed the street had been a mistake. She jogged two steps, grabbed his arm, and steered him in the direction of the empty driveway house.

A white piece of paper taped to the front door fluttered in the wind. All they needed to do was stand on the stoop for a couple of minutes and pretend to ring the bell. They'd leave once someone came to the door.

Once they mounted the one step to the stoop, it was easier to see the paper, which Gus chose to read aloud. "Don't bother knocking. We're too broke to buy anything. We don't need to find Jesus. We've already picked our political candidates. We don't need new windows. Did you miss the part about us being broke? Go away!"

He laughed, nudged Eunice, and commented. "Sounds a bit like you, huh?"

"No!" she snapped her response, while mentally admitting some parts of it did sound like her. Back when she was in her own house, she did answer the door, mainly because she ordered things. It was always a disappointment when someone wanted to give her a home improvement spiel or have her sign a petition. At least at Greener Pastures, she didn't have to be worried about that. They stood staring at the door for a minute, then Eunice pushed the doorbell.

Gus turned his head, his brow wrinkled more than usual, and asked, "Why did you do that?"

"Because I could." A slight smile lifted the corner of her lips.

"You know whoever lives here won't answer or when they do, they won't be happy."

A twitch of the curtains indicated there was indeed someone home, which caused Eunice to exclaim, "Not my problem!" as she exited the stoop and walked across the lawn to get to the next house. Gus caught up to her when she reached the grass-cutting-on-Sunday neighbors' house. Luck was with them. No one was home.

Gus clapped his hands together. "Looks like we're done. Maybe we can get Herman to take us to that fish place for lunch. I'm so hungry my belly is making acquaintance with my backbone."

A snack or a meal sounded like a good bet. Eunice was sure the others would agree. With her luck, Lola would try to work in a trip to the drugstore to buy more makeup, which Herman would agree to since he was sweet on the woman. Speaking of Herman, Eunice put her hands on her hips and slowly pivoted, searching for Herman and his car. Normally, her eyes weren't much of an issue. However, there was a big difference between having trouble reading the small print on a bottle and missing an entire car. "Um, Gus? Do you see Herman or his car?"

Using his flattened hand as a sunshade, Gus peered into the distance and pointed. "There's Lance's house. No car."

"Yeah," she agreed and inwardly gave a sigh of relief, happy her eyesight wasn't that bad. Then reality came crashing down on her. Herman was gone. Had he decided to play a trick on them? She may have teased him a time or two, but a person should be able to take a joke. Thank goodness she had her phone and could call a car with her app. Unfortunately, it was billed to her daughter's account, and she'd know about her adventure. After hiding in Herman's car when he and his friends decided to head to North Carolina, her daughter threatened to put her into a more secure facility, which would basically be a prison. However, the center promised to keep a better eye on her. She was moved to a locked door wing, but nothing stopped her from walking to the other wings to exit.

"Gus, if I have to call for a car, this might be it. Somehow, I managed to convince my daughter that my last Uber ride was a billing mistake. Another *billing mistake*, and I might end up living with my daughter." She trembled as if chilled. Most adult children worry about their parents coming to live with them, but it was the opposite with Eunice. Any fun or adventure was missing from her daughter, who epitomized the words *organized* and *boring*. Images of sitting in a clean room with a locked window and her daughter handing her a printed schedule with everything from meal times to bedtime printed on it made her groan audibly.

"Don't take on so. Lola is still here. No way would Herman leave her. I think I see Jake farther up, too."

Shaking off what could happen, she surveyed the street and found a wild patch of color in between all the green lawns and shrubs. *Lola.* This was probably the first time in her life she was happy to see her vivid wardrobe. Farther up and a little harder to see was the rangy figure of Jake, who was waving one arm. "Do you think he's waving at us?"

"Huh?"

He didn't hear her that time but heard her just fine the other times. Eunice knew it would do her no good to mention it. Gus liked playing practical jokes. Not being able to hear could be one of them, or it could be only one of his ears was bad. The two of them walked up the street and met Lola on the way. Their original intentions of not being seen together were forgotten in their intent on finding Herman and the car. When they reached Jake, he grinned and pointed to a short jog of a street that connected the two main streets in the neighborhood. As the four of them strolled in that direction, they saw Herman standing outside his car with a map spread out on the hood.

Upon spotting them, he pulled out a handkerchief and wiped his brow. "Thank goodness you're back. I can only be confused about where I'm going for so long. I had to leave the first street after a man gave me directions. It would have just been weird to stick around. I told Jake where I was, but I've been here fifteen minutes or so, staring at my map in full view, and no one has offered to help me. Whatever happened to caring about your fellow man?"

Gus harrumphed while Jake skirted the hood of the car and stared at the map. "Good thing no one tried to come out and assist you."

"Why not?" Herman queried. "I look harmless enough."

"Yes," Lola agreed with a nod. "He reminds me a little of Santa Claus."

Herman's bushy white eyebrows went up with the proclamation as he waited for clarification. "And...?"

"Without the beard," Lola continued.

This made Gus laugh. "Notice she said nothing about the belly." He tried to pat Herman's stomach, but Herman swatted his hand away.

Jake folded the map up and handed it to Herman with the name of the map prominently displayed. "If someone *had* tried to help you, it may have been a wee bit suspicious since you're using a North Carolina map in Indiana."

The four of them climbed into the car and chuckled as they did so. Herman remained silent as he took his place behind the wheel and started the car. He checked the rearview mirror and asked, "What did you hotshots find out?"

Jake cleared his throat before speaking. "I'd like a different cover. No one wants to subscribe to the local paper. Apparently, the competing paper across the river is offering gifts to subscribers. I had one person ask me what her gift would be."

"I bet you told her absolutely nothing," Lola commented, with amusement coloring her words.

"Should have," Jake admitted. He blew out a long breath. "Instead, I gave her the unopened beef jerky I was saving for a snack. She told me it wasn't enough to get her to subscribe to the paper, and she *also* kept my beef jerky. I wouldn't mind going somewhere for a bite to eat."

The car moved forward as Herman shifted into drive, leisurely left the neighborhood, and turned right. "I wouldn't mind a sugar cookie or some hot cocoa. Guess I'll have to head up to the North Pole and feed the reindeer first."

Lola leaned as far toward Herman as her seatbelt would allow and cooed, "Being compared to Santa Claus is a compliment. Everyone loves him. Besides, I find his beard kinda sexy. Ever thought of growing a beard to go with your magnificent mustache?"

Things were going south in a hurry. Eunice rolled the window down and tried to stick her head out to get away from all the mushy talk. "Stop, please. We have a case to solve."

Her exclamation got the sleuths talking about more than Herman's resemblance to Santa Claus and Jake losing beef jerky to a non-newspaper subscriber. Jake and Herman had zilch while Lola contributed that the missing Loretta had sold make-up and toiletries on the side. According to one neighbor, she was a walking billboard for her product.

Eunice added the second-hand information given by Hazel that Loretta was a yeller and a *colorful* individual. Sometimes, the use of the word colorful could mean a variety of things from salty language, vivid wardrobe, or just plain weird.

"Okay," Eunice announced, holding up one finger that those in the front seat could not see. "We have a woman who is loud, wears too much makeup, may have a garish wardrobe, and could curse a great deal. She shouldn't be too hard to find. How many women can there be like that?"

She made a point of staring at Lola, who refused to rise to the bait. Instead, Herman did. "Have you even glanced out the window?"

While they had been talking, Herman maneuvered the car onto a busy street thick with traffic, strip malls, and fast-food restaurants. Strolling, a few standing, and some more yelling into cell phones were women in bright clothing and wearing too much makeup. Since her window was still down, it was easy to tell some were loud talkers and a few used colorful language, too.

Why did everything have to be so hard? Eunice lifted her chin. On the other hand, hard wasn't impossible.

Chapter Five

DARK CLOUDS GATHERED on the horizon as the senior sleuths exited the chicken restaurant. Herman licked his fingers. "Boy, that was good. Reminds me of when I lived back in Legacy. My neighbor, Donna…"

Every one of the sleuths had heard in detail about Herman's old neighbor who ran a B and B. No matter how good food was, nothing could compare to Donna's dishes. Eunice was tired of Herman's constant bragging, taking the shine off a perfectly good meal.

"Please, not again. We all know that Donna is the best cook on the planet."

"Maybe not the best, but pretty close."

Gus, who had been the recipient of some of Donna's dishes, rubbed his belly. "That woman knows her way around pies and pretty much every other dessert."

Eunice sighed. This wasn't going the way she wanted. Personally, she'd rather not think about her trip to Legacy. It brought back memories of her daughter swooping in and carting her back to the center like a naughty toddler. If that wasn't bad enough, she had to listen to the boys talk about what a great time they had coming back. Truthfully, they hadn't fared much better since they were escorted home by Detective Tabor, the new bridegroom, for safety reasons. It could have been Jake's speeding or Gus knocking a hole in the hotel wall that may have made the veteran detective doubtful of their abilities.

Many times, when people saw the elderly, they imagined used up folks with no hopes or dreams, who were content watching endless reruns. Her eyes narrowed and her step grew more forceful. Maybe she didn't have a full head of lustrous hair or a tight rear, but she could run mental circles around some of the younger employees at the center who depended on their cell phone to tell them everything.

Gus cleared his throat, then asked, "What's got you stomping around? You didn't have to order the chicken livers."

He didn't see it or maybe not as well as she did. "I *wanted* the chicken livers," she answered, snapping the words. The man stumbled back and placed a hand over his heart as if she had mortally wounded him, which made his friends chuckle, but just made Eunice uncomfortable.

It was fortunate she married the first man who asked her because apparently there were not many suitors waiting in line. Her grandmother cautioned her to accept the proposal because there might not be any more in the offing due to her personality. As one gentleman caller put it, she could be a trifle acerbic. After that caller had made his final goodbye, she went inside and looked up *acerbic*, which had more than one meaning. The first was a sharp and forthright way of speaking, which she took as a compliment. The second was bitter or sour tasting.

It made her wonder if the years she spent in the furniture business had made her difficult to be around or were most men yellow livered nincompoops who couldn't abide a strong woman? It had to be the latter. Still, available men were few and far between at

Greener Pastures, and she knew good and well there were a couple of floozies who had their eyes on her man. It would pay to be less acerbic.

"Um, I didn't mean to yell at you. It's just I was thinking about how people don't take, um…" She hesitated, not wanting to say the word elderly since it had so many bad connotations. "…mature folks like ourselves seriously."

Gus gave her a searching look as if he understood, then laughed.

Drat him. Just when she thought he might not have a sensitive soul underneath all his tomfoolery, he reached for her hand and entwined his fingers with hers. A major move on his part since Gus wasn't known for public shows of affection. Sometimes, when they were watching television in either of their rooms, he *might* hold her hand.

He gave her hand a little squeeze before speaking. "I'm not sure there was a time in my life when people did take me seriously. When I was a kid, my parents told me I didn't know anything. As a soldier, I constantly took orders from those who were older. As a young father and husband, I had my in-laws to tell me how everything was done and how I was making a mess of it."

Herman chimed in. "I hear ya."

Knowing which part, he was agreeing to was difficult since Herman had never been married. They reached the car, and Herman made a show of opening the door for Lola and stowing her walker in the trunk.

Not dissuaded by the interruption or possibly not hearing it, Gus continued, "You can't let those who want to tell you how to do things or refuse to listen to you get you down. I figured out a long time ago, there were two kinds of people in this world—the workers and the royals. The royals sit around and give orders on how to do things they have never done in their entire lives. The workers get the job done by often ignoring the royals. You and I are the workers. We're going to find Loretta if only to show that we of a certain age are able."

It made sense. Eunice glanced down at their hands and smiled. Here she went after Gus just because she thought he was cute. Who knew he could be so insightful?

Jake slapped the top of the sedan. "You done speechifying yet? We got places to go."

They really didn't. They were headed back to the center unless they made a side trip to the drugstore, which they probably would. It wouldn't be the worst thing. It would give her a chance to stock up on candy and celebrity gossip. Unlike most who bought the magazines and gushed over the celebrities and their extravagant lifestyles, Eunice enjoyed reading about the stupid things they did. Their fans never considered their heartthrobs' actions stupid, but they weren't thinking with a clear head. Sometimes, seeing those who were idolized playing the fool made her feel like the last thinking person on the planet. She knew it wasn't true, but it was almost the same joy as biting into a nougaty candy bar. The candy bar was better.

THIRTY MINUTES LATER, they climbed back into the car after what was supposed to be a short trip to the drugstore. Gus bought a cigar and was offended they didn't ask for his ID.

Herman turned to address the backseat occupants. "There will be no smoking in my car." As if there was any question to whom he was talking, Herman waved his finger in Gus's direction. "That means you."

"Come on, be a sport," Gus said. "You know they won't let me smoke it at the center."

"Not my problem," Herman replied as he buckled his seatbelt and started the car. "Should have thought of that before you bought it."

On that point, Eunice had to agree. Her seatmate, Gus, elbowed her and mouthed the word royal. Contrary to what he said before about the royals doing nothing, it must refer to anyone who disagrees with you, too. Gus and she had been keeping company for the last couple of months, which meant she knew he'd smoke that cigar no matter what. It wasn't like he was hooked on smoking, but more on doing something when he was told he couldn't. Her sweetie was a bad boy.

After patting down his chest and pants pockets, Gus turned to Jake. "You got a light?"

"Why would I have a light? I don't smoke, and I'm not planning on starting a fire or lighting candles for a romantic dinner."

"Gus—" Herman started but was interrupted by Lola.

"Ah, Jake, no romantic candlelit dinners. Several ladies I know will be disappointed. Candlelight is much kinder to older skin."

Even though her normal response would be to say something to the effect that Lola would be one to know, Eunice held herself back. This team needed to be on task. "Enough of the cigars and candlelight. Let's talk about Loretta. It's obvious by the loud arguments the neighbors heard that Loretta wasn't happy."

There was a general murmur of agreement.

"What do unhappy wives do?" Eunice prompted.

"Kill their husbands," Lola interjected, not even hesitating for a second.

On a normal day, Eunice would have pried, but as far as she knew, Lola had never been married. It must have been some of her showgirl friends that did away with their husbands or maybe one too many police dramas. "Her husband is still alive."

"Nags him to death," Gus offered by her side.

She pursed her lips and cut her eyes to her companion. Was he trying to imply that she nagged him? Ridiculous. "I repeat, the husband is still alive."

"Then…" Jake held up his hand. "…your only other options are leaving, taking up with another man, and leaving with the man she just took up with."

Eunice's hand clap resonated through the car. "You got it! Glad to see someone is thinking out of the box here. Lance trusts the man so he must be trustworthy."

On their outings, Herman usually concentrated on driving with the occasional request for directions from the locals. "Don't be so sure about that, kids. Every time they finally nail a serial killer, they interview the neighbors who talk about what a nice man he was and how they had no clue."

He had her there. Gus might not like to be told no, but it was nothing compared to Eunice's refusal not to be right. She'd rewrite history books if need be. Heaven knows most of that stuff was made up anyhow. George Washington did not chop down a cherry tree or throw a coin across the Potomac River. He certainly hadn't been standing up in a boat as his portrait showed. Only a fool does that.

He would have ended up tipping the boat over, to die from drowning or hypothermia.

She rolled her eyes, although no one was looking at her to notice. "Seriously, people say that stuff to cover their own guilt. I'm sure behind closed doors they *did* talk about how weird their neighbor was. Look at how much information we as total strangers got today. Of course, Lance's neighbor hasn't been declared a serial killer. If he were, Hazel would be singing a different story about she hadn't an inkling something nefarious was going on in the house down the street or that a possible killer resided there. Those who know or even suspect are usually guilty by association. No one is going to say they thought the man was a bloodthirsty murderer. Instead, they might say they heard a scream but assumed he had the television up too loud."

"I never thought of it that way," Lola said with a nod. "You have a valid point."

Drat. She hated it when Lola agreed with her, especially since she had made a point of disliking the former showgirl. After all, everyone else liked her. Her faded glamor attracted both male and female residents. More than a few employees wanted to know what it was like to be a Vegas showgirl. No one ever asked her what it was like to work in a furniture warehouse, despite her business knowledge helping them solve a previous case.

In the world of Greener Pastures, Lola was the cheerleader while Eunice was the—she struggled for a word that would describe her place. She wasn't the nerd, the scholar, or the jock. In her real-life high school, some bonehead boy had nicknamed her mosquito because she was always buzzing around and making noise. The dullard had no clue that it was the male mosquitoes that buzzed and the females were the ones who bit you. Yeah, that wasn't something she'd ever bring up.

Herman had made his way back to the home with ease. They pulled into the back parking lot where they could enter without being noticed. She had to give the man points for thinking of parking in the employee parking space. No one would look twice at a car entering or leaving staff parking. While Herman could come and go as he pleased, it wasn't as easy for the rest of them, especially her, since she was on twenty-four watch to prevent escape even if the staff had relaxed their observation after a couple of weeks. Thank goodness for that.

Since it would be a hike to go in the wing entrance, they made a point of checking the side entrance the employees used, which was right next to the time clock. Most didn't bother to secure the door, which she hoped held true this time. After all, they put in enough exercise canvassing the neighborhood. It took them a few minutes to unload, but then they headed toward the door where a half-grown black and white cat waited. It gave a plaintive *meow* as they approached.

"Oh, look," Lola cooed. "A kitty. I heard talk about the center getting a cat. I wonder if this is the wing cat, and it escaped?"

Eunice reached the door first. Glory of glories, it was unlocked. She pulled the door open and the cat darted in. Well, it looked like Greener Pastures now had another resident cat. The rest of them shuffled in after her, talking about what they would do for the rest of the day. Although she would never admit it, the day had tired her. A nap would be just the thing. Since her reputation was all about her endless energy, she hated to admit to a lack of it.

"See ya." She waved at Gus before she hustled toward her wing. The sounds of bingo numbers being called came from the activity room. No temptation there, especially when she could hear her pillow calling her name. Television programs leaked into the corridor from doors that were ajar. The residents managed to appear busy while accepting visitors with the partially opened door. Since some doors didn't have locks, there was a door etiquette.

A trio of women with rouge red cheeks, reeking of perfume, popped out of one room. Even though she'd suspected one of making eyes previously at Gus, she didn't bother to engage her and breezed past, possibly leaving the women open-mouthed in her wake. Just getting into her room and closing her door sounded better and better.

Ahead of her, a staff employee in a brightly colored tunic stood talking to a man and woman in square dance costumes. They should have left by now. *Weird.* She tried to dodge around the three, but hearing her name brought her up short.

"Eunice is great about getting things started. I can really depend on her. Hey, Eunice! Come on over here and meet Bob and Debbi. They're the leaders of Happy Feet Square Dancing and Clogging Squadron."

Even though she loved the compliments, she knew she was being played. It was a trap to get her to do work without pay. "Hi, Bob and Debbi. Great show. I know nothing about square dancing, but Herman does." She nodded at the activity director and grinned. "If it involves square dancing, then he's your guy."

She waved, then left as quick as she could before any more questions could be asked. She may have gotten Herman roped into something he didn't want to do, but the man could always say no. In many ways, Herman was similar to her stray cat. They both had survival instincts. Everyone did. It was unfortunate most forgot how to use theirs.

Chapter Six

THE CENTER DIMMED the lights after nine in the evening, certain the residents were in bed or at least in their rooms. Even though most could see well enough to move down the corridors, it did nothing to illuminate the edges of the wall, corners, or crevices where a cat might hide. Eunice clutched the napkin-wrapped fish she saved from her supper. After tossing Herman under the bus when the activity director was hunting for volunteers, she kept to her room. When she wasn't thinking about the center's newest furry resident, she regretted suggesting Herman.

She narrowed her eyes and peeked behind a potted plant where she saw a suspicious shadow. Too round to be a cat, and it wasn't moving. She poked at it with the edge of her foot, making it roll. A yarn ball unraveled a little as it traveled across the floor. It easily could have been dropped by a resident, and Domino could have played with it.

Mentally, she had been trying out names for her new cat. There was also Oreo or Fred Astaire because his black and white coat resembled formal wear. She hadn't decided on one name, yet. It all depended on her chance-found feline remaining at the center.

Personally, she'd like to have her own pet as opposed to a group pet that so many would fuss over. If that happened, she'd never get a chance to sit with a cat in her lap. A street cat might not take to lap sitting, but if she socialized it, there might be a chance. One thing she did know—when she set her mind to something, it got done.

In the lobby, she peered behind the furniture and called in a low voice, "Here kitty, kitty."

The squeak of rubber-soled shoes on the freshly waxed floor meant Eunice wasn't the only one in the vicinity. The rapid stride meant it wasn't a resident. A woman's voice called out, "Who's there?"

Oh great. She pressed her lips together to stop the snort behind her teeth. Eunice straightened to see who might be addressing her. The woman stepped closer, allowing the overhead light to reveal the well-padded figure and flamboyant blonde hairdo. It was the new aide, Misty. Just her luck, she'd meet a staffer who was on work probation and anxious to prove herself. Most of the other employees wouldn't have bothered to investigate. Truth worked well, especially when flavored with the listener's mistaken beliefs. "I was looking for my cat. When I was five, my father brought home a kitten for me that he had found at…"

"Never mind," Misty replied, with a smirk teasing at the corners of her mouth. "Good luck finding your cat." She returned to walking in the direction of the staff lounge.

Technically, Eunice hadn't lied. She did receive a kitten when she was five, but she also played into the belief that most of the residents were living in the past. If Misty only knew how much in the present she was and what a mover and shaker she was in the center. Her forehead furrowed even more when she considered Herman trying to interest people in square dancing. There might be more than a few who might be interested in dancing, but she couldn't depend on Herman to flush out the possible dancers.

"Gotta do it myself," she grumbled. She was well aware no one was listening besides herself. Still, it made her feel more in charge to talk to herself. It used to be if people talked to themselves, folks would think they were a bit daft. Fortunately, Eunice kept up with the news via the various newspapers the center subscribed to. Scientists recently put out that folks who talked to their pets were possibly more stable than those who didn't. Even Einstein carried on conversations with himself. Who knows? Maybe she was a genius, too?

No sign of the cat in her wing or the lobby, which would be quite a distance for the feline to travel without being seen. Since she chose to dine in her room like a coward, she had missed out on the recent gossip. All this sneaking around may be a waste if someone had spotted the cat and put it outside, or worse. Eunice placed her hand on her chest as she pondered the possibility.

"Someone took my cat!"

She dropped the hand that rested over her heart as her eyes narrowed. "That Marjorie has my cat. It's just like her." Eunice turned slowly as if expecting the mentioned woman to appear with the cat in her arms. The corridor remained empty and silent except for the furnace hum. Well, that proved nothing. All she could do was continue to look.

The sound of canned laughter slid under the closed resident's doors as Eunice turned into a different corridor. She stayed away from the nurse's station. There was bound to be one or more employees there. While the residents were free to roam the building, Eunice tried to keep her appearance low-key. Not attracting too much attention while looking for her forbidden feline would be better.

If she had help, the search might go faster. Of course, it would mean letting someone in on her secret. The best way to keep a secret was if the only other of the holders of the information was dead. Well, that wouldn't serve. Gus would probably help. Knowing Gus, he'd forget and spill the beans at the worst time. A heavy sigh escaped her lips. It *would* be better than lurking in the corridor alone like a bad odor.

A few turns and one step back into the shadow of a doorway kept her presence hidden as she worked her way to Gus's room. His door was slightly ajar, and she pushed it wide. He was staring at something on his desk. His intent gaze amused her, and she asked, "What's caught your interest?"

No response. She moved farther into the room and leaned over and touched his arm, startling him.

"Ah!" Gus exhaled the word and jumped the slightest bit. He snapped his gaze to Eunice. "Good heavens, woman. Are you trying to give me a heart attack?"

"No. Far from it. What are you looking at?"

He gestured to a paper on his desk covered in bold writing: a copy of Loretta's letter warning that if she disappeared to suspect her husband. "Curious, if you ask me."

"Why is that?" She picked up the paper and read it aloud. "*Dear Police. I have reason to believe my husband may harm me. He has done everything he could to make my life as bland as possible. He's resisted my every action to bring color and joy into our existence. I don't believe I can live like this any longer. He refuses to let me live any other way. If I should disappear, make sure to check out my husband. He may appear to be a mild-mannered man, but those are the worst. Please do this for me. Loretta.*"

She shook her head and placed the letter back on the desk. "It's a peculiar letter for sure. It sounds more like she was dying from boredom."

"True enough," Gus agreed and turned to look at the letters. "That's not what I was looking at though. It's the handwriting."

Even though she had read the letter, Eunice took another peek at it. "It's fancy. Might even call it flamboyant. A gal has to practice quite a bit to have writing like that. Probably took pride in her handwriting."

"Yep." Gus picked up the paper and waved it. "Can you imagine someone penning something so fancy when she was in fear of her life or ready to dart off to a new one?"

It was a fair question. She tried to imagine the woman trembling as she made the decision to flee. Maybe she ran through the house, throwing things into a duffle bag. Maybe she wrote the note on her way out or sitting in the post office parking lot. She held out her hand. "Let me see that letter again."

It burnt her good that Gus could find something she missed. Of course, if she hadn't been hiding in her room to avoid Herman, she'd have been a part of the brainstorming. She might have uncovered the information before Gus did. Her lips twisted to one side. Then again, she might have missed it all, concerned about her missing kitty. Now that she had the letter in her hand, her gaze fixed on it. She noticed the steady stream of letters marching across the page. There was no hesitation in composing the letter. It was as if she already knew what she was going to say.

"There's no stopping and starting. It was like she just sat down and wrote it out. Like she had thought it out on her own." Eunice pointed to the body of the letter.

"Maybe her husband isn't a bad guy at all. Could be Loretta is living it up somewhere."

That was pretty much what the neighbors thought. It would be the easy answer. Still, it made her wonder why no one had heard from Loretta. If she had moved on to another state and had become a success—whatever that meant to her—it would be hard for the woman not to gloat. Eunice would have found a way to make her triumph known. "It's odd no one has heard from her."

Gus arched his bushy eyebrows. "Maybe someone has. We just haven't asked the right people."

Another possible insight from her sweetie, which meant she was off her game. She swallowed hard since the words she needed to say were difficult to utter. "You're right. We need to look into this. Lance might share if a paper trail is attached to our fancy letter writer. That's not why I stopped by, though."

Gus cleared his throat and winked. "I bet you missed my handsome self."

While that wasn't the real reason, she knew enough not to be too honest. Men tended to get all blustery and difficult when you didn't agree with their own praise. "You know me. I can't keep away from you. Oh, and there's another matter you might be able to help me with."

Chapter Seven

THE WINDOWED DINING doors allowed residents to peek in to see what was going on before entering, but they let in meager light. A high-pitched squeak had Gus and Eunice hurrying in the direction of the kitchen where the stainless-steel appliances reflected the limited illumination. A slew of red lights at various work stations showed the electrical appliances were plugged in and sucking down their nightly energy supplement. It also gave a macabre red cast to the scene. Even though it wasn't much, it was enough to notice a black and white cat clutching a squirming mouse in its mouth.

Eunice took an involuntary step back, bumping into Gus. She clapped her hands once and ordered, "Drop it, Oscar!"

It could have been the surprise of observers or even being addressed that caused the cat to drop the still live mouse, which shot into the shadows. The cat glanced back at Eunice reproachfully before taking off in the same direction as the mouse.

"No!" Eunice yelped. She half-turned and grabbed Gus's arm. "Do something. We can't have my cat living on a diet of rodents."

Her words had done nothing to nudge her gentleman caller into action. "Aren't you worried about the cat getting some disease from eating mice?" she demanded "They carry parasites, maybe even the plague. We can't have the plague returning."

Gus sighed and wrapped his arm around Eunice's thin shoulders before he spoke. "You realize modern medicine wiped out the plague. We should be more alarmed that we have mice in the kitchen."

It sounded like he was doing nothing. *Geesh.* While she did enjoy the feel of his arm around her shoulders, it looked like she was going to have to rescue the cat on her own. A large *crash*, followed by several smaller metallic tings alerted her to the location of her kitty. Before she could move, a mouse ran across her feet, followed by her cat. A quick response had her jogging after the two.

Light flooded the kitchen as Eunice turned the corner into the pantry. An irate voice asked from a distance, "What are you doing here?"

Eunice closed the pantry door quietly, locking herself in the dark with the cat, mouse, about one hundred number-10 cans of Blue Lake green beans, applesauce, and countless bags of rice, but away from the inquisitor. The strong smell of onions practically gagged her as she put her ear to the crack of the door to follow the conversation.

"Ah," Gus stalled, possibly wondering where his girlfriend went. "I wanted a snack."

"You have a kitchenette in your room where you can store plenty of snacks. Even if your cupboard was bare, you should ask a nurse for a snack. I know they have pudding cups, crackers, and cookies at their station."

Good point. Eunice wondered how Gus would handle it. He cleared his throat. "Yeah, that. I don't want that stuff. I'm trying to eat healthier. I was hoping to find a nice apple or turnip or something."

A disbelieving snort sounded. "You're out of luck. The fridges are all locked. Trust me, I know. Go back to your room."

"I will. I think I should clean up my mess first."

Good boy. He was making an excuse to stay behind to check on her. Gus always was a stand-up kind of guy. A swelling of appreciation filled her heart as she tried to ignore the sounds of scurrying behind her. It sounded like more than one mouse to her. Not something she wanted to think about. An anonymous call to the board of health might be in order. If nothing else, she could push a note under the dietician's door to alert her to the problem.

"No," the no-nonsense staffer insisted. "You're leaving, and I'm locking up the dining room."

"That's mighty unfriendly," Gus objected in an aggrieved tone. "This is folks' home. What are they going to think when they see the doors locked?"

Yeah, Eunice silently asserted. *You tell her.*

There was no more conversation and only the sound of retreating footsteps. There was a firm slam of the doors. Good gracious. They were leaving her *and* locking her in. She couldn't believe it. Her hands tightened into fists as she considered her quandary. Well, she had done it now. She took five slow breaths, waiting for anyone who was nearby to slip away before she snapped on the light.

The brightness had her squeezing her eyes shut until she felt able to open them. Around her were shelves of foodstuff with a narrow alley in between. It was her guess that only young, skinny employees were ever sent back into the pantry. Good thing she wasn't claustrophobic. A soft plop revealed her feline weaving his way through the pork-n-beans. He managed to knock off a can that landed with a thud. Weren't cats supposed to be graceful? Apparently, this one had issues. She watched the cat work his way over the food items from the corner of her eye. As long as he thought she wasn't looking, he might draw closer.

She waited, holding her breath, watching the flash of the black and white feline make its way toward the door. *Almost there—keep coming kitty,* she mentally urged. In a lightning move that not only surprised the cat but Eunice, too, she scooped up the cat. Ever the ingrate, it wiggled and tried to escape, causing her to tighten her hold a little.

Okay, she was in a locked kitchen. No, wait. The bossy employee had locked the dining room. She didn't mention the dietician's office, which opened into the kitchen. Sure, the exterior door was probably locked from the outside but could be opened from the inside. At least, she hoped it worked that way.

Eunice slipped out of the panty, turning out the light and pulling the door shut. The mice might feast for the night, but their time would be short after she penned a note to the dietician. After all, she had just sealed up the evidence in the pantry. Too bad she couldn't solve the case of the vanishing wife as easily.

She popped out of the dietician's office with the cat under one arm. *Drat.* She lost her napkin-wrapped fish in the process. There were a couple cans of tuna in her kitchen cabinet.

Gus, not paying attention, peered through the dining room door windows and muttered to himself. "She's going to kill me."

"No, she's not," Eunice assured him.

A grin lit up her face as Gus spun around, managing to look both shocked and delighted. "You got out!"

"Obviously. Let's get this cat back to my room." Even though it wouldn't be that long of a walk, two residents would appear less suspicious than one lone resident. Gus had on a cardigan, which gave her the idea. "Can you place your sweater around my shoulders?"

"You cold?" Gus peeled off his sweater and placed it on Eunice's shoulders. "Better?"

The man's sweater was already a little big on Gus, so it hung loose on Eunice, covering the cat's tail and head. Unfortunately, it kept squirming, giving the appearance of an energetic hand muff. "If we hurry and keep talking, we should be fine."

They hustled down the hall, talking in low voices. Every now and then, a plaintive meow would sound. If Misty showed up, she would want to be overly helpful and would notice the cat or at least hear its call. "Gus? Could you throw a meow in every now and then?"

"I think I know how Herman must have felt when they smuggled in Bear. Geesh. Some aide thought Herman was barking. Now, people will start talking about *me*."

"Not unless you start meowing all the time."

The squeak of rubber-soled shoes came up from behind. A woman's voice queried, "What are you two doing out roaming the halls?"

"*Now!*" Eunice hissed to her companion.

"Meow, meow, meow," Gus replied. "That's what she said to me. Then, I said meow, meow yourself."

The nurse moved around them, barely looking at them, but added in passing, "If you're going to drink, you need to stay in your room."

"Meow," offered the unnamed cat.

"Room!" the nurse insisted before disappearing down an intersecting corridor.

"Did you hear that?" Gus asked in a miffed voice. "She thinks I'm drunk."

"Better than her thinking you're crazy."

"I guess," Gus agreed, but still folded his arms and jutted out his chin. "Why the name Oscar? Old boyfriend?"

"Old cat." *Darn.* She had just missed an opportunity to tease the man with past boyfriends—not that there had been that many. "I'm trying out names. I haven't decided on one yet."

"The name Trouble sounds right to me."

"Of course, you'd say that." She gestured to her room door. "We're here."

The three of them slipped into the room. Eunice turned on the television to disguise any random meows. "I need to get my furry friend some food since I dropped the fish in the kitchen."

"You also deprived it of a mouse dinner," Gus reminded in a joking manner.

After a short search, Eunice located a couple of small bowls and the tuna. One bowl she filled with water. The other she scooped tuna into and placed it on the floor. "Here ya go."

The cat, who had been investigating the corners of the room, came over to check out the offering. He gave it a couple of sniffs, then settled down to eat, purring while he did so.

"I'm going to need some cat supplies," Eunice said more to herself than to Gus.

It didn't stop her friend from responding. "I imagine you can order some online, but you will need a litter box and litter right away" He made a face. "You know what that means."

Oh yes, she did. Normally, Eunice's mode of living was full speed ahead, and everyone needed to get out of her way. After becoming part of the Senior Sleuths, she realized the practicality of working with others. It wasn't like she had made the transition to plays well with others quite yet. "I have to make up with Herman to get him to drive me around."

"Yep," Gus agreed with a nod.

A simple apology wouldn't serve. Some people might call her a grudge holder. Come to think of it, most people did. Herman could hold one longer than she did. "Any suggestions on how to sweeten up the man?"

Gus pressed his hand to his heart. "Oh, that look would do it for me. However, it won't work on Herman. Lola might get upset, too, thinking you're sweet on her man. No, it has to be something big since you somehow got him named Square Dance Chairman."

It wasn't too hard to see where this was going. A commercial came on featuring a woman petting her contented cat, saying nothing was too good for her pet. Sacrifices had to be made to have a pet, especially covert pets.

Her hand went up to rub the bridge of her nose. "I know nothing about square dancing. It's the reason I suggested Herman."

Gus settled for a disbelieving look before sitting down on a kitchenette chair. "Come on. You expect me to believe you didn't do it to nettle Herman a little?"

Actually, she had. Keeping her thumb and forefinger about an inch apart, she confided, "A tiny bit. I like the idea of square dancing, but I know nothing about it."

Gus interlaced his fingers and rested his chin in them briefly before speaking. "If you hadn't taken off like a scalded cat…" He nodded to the cat, "My apologies. It's just an expression. Anyhow, I could have told you I know all about square dancing. My deceased wife was a great square dancer, and she taught me. I could teach you."

A mental starting gun sounded in Eunice's head as she grabbed onto the words, "*my deceased wife was a great square dancer*". Her competitive side insisted she'd be better. "Challenge accepted."

"What?" Gus blinked at her.

Either he didn't hear her or didn't understand what she meant. Typical. "I said I'd let you be my Square Dance Co-Chairperson."

Chapter Eight

THE AIDES ELBOWED each other when Gus and Eunice requested breakfast in her room as opposed to going to the dining room. A snicker popped out of one while the other managed to contain hers.

"Uh-huh." The younger aide waggled her brows and smirked. "I can do that." She cut her eyes to the other aide and shared a meaningful look. "I hope to have half your energy when I'm your age."

Eunice gave a derisive sniff. "You'll have to start eating better then." She pivoted to return to her room, missing whatever look or comment the aide had to make. The door closed behind her. Gus coughed and looked up from his place in the easy chair where he sat petting the cat.

"Asking for breakfast for both of us will cause talk."

He acted like she wasn't aware the center was a gossip mill churning out rumors based on the tiniest string of events or words. After all, she had done her part starting a few of them. Eunice crossed her arms and gave her beau an indulgent look. The man didn't know how to be wily. Most men didn't. They just came out and demanded what they wanted. If they didn't get it, they raised their voices. Females, especially those of her generation, had to learn to know when to ask and occasionally manipulate the situation to suit their purposes.

"I know what they'll think. All the better because it will keep them out of my room and discovering Jinx."

Gus's hand hovered in midair, right above the feline. "Ah. I see. You *are* clever." He continuing to pet the cat. "Not sure about the name Jinx. Seems to me like it's inviting trouble. How about Checkers?"

"Are you kidding me?" How could her sweetie miss the obvious? Sometimes, she wondered why she even hung out with the man. The women residents outnumbered the men five to one. Never mind, though. He was probably the only male who would put up with her. Her lips tugged upward as she gazed at the baffled expression on Gus's face. She loved that expression. "Checkers are black and red."

"Oh yeah. I forgot about that. You're right. Maybe I was thinking about chess. I don't think that would be a good name, either. What do you think?"

"No." Already tired of the subject, Eunice turned to the cabinets to locate the tuna. "We're going to have to get Herman to take us to the store."

"Ha! You honked him off. You'll do the begging," Gus insisted with a twinkle in his eye.

She suspected Gus might see things that way. "I'll accept that I'm at fault." Her lips pursed as she considered the situation. "I don't think a simple apology will suffice."

Apologies were not something she did well, and Herman wouldn't make it easy, of that she was sure. Come to think of it, she may have never apologized where she actually meant it. Quite frankly, it was not her way. The cat lifted his furry head and gave a plaintive meow. Ah yes. She needed a reminder of why she had to grovel.

There was a knock before the door swung open. Not enough time to hide the feline. Instead, Eunice went with the ploy that worked in so many movies. She leaned over Gus, bracing herself on the chair arms while dipping her head to kiss him.

Her body hid her furry friend, but surprised Gus who blurted, "What are you doing?"

A dietary aid deposited the food trays and snorted. "Honey, if you have no clue, I can't help you."

The woman left promptly, which worked out well because the cat squeezed out between the two of them. His paws allowed a soft landing on the floor. The indignant swish of his tail announced his feeling about the whole matter.

Eunice managed to push off the chair arms with some effort, but her balance was unstable. She fell into Gus's lap as the aide re-entered the room, holding up a carton of chocolate milk. "I forgot your chocolate milk. I know how you feel about it." She gave the two of them an interesting glance and raised her eyebrows. "I'll close the door on my way out. Figure you might appreciate that."

Eunice stared at the closed door, certain the woman may have pretended to care about her privacy, but even now was gossiping with her co-workers. As far as closing the door, she did it because she didn't want to be overheard. The good news was there was no mention of a cat. Apparently, the feline's survival instinct kicked in, and it had found a hiding place.

What a clever animal! Eunice silently congratulated the animal as her eyes scanned the room for it. The black and white cat was perched on the kitchen counter, leisurely eating off one of the breakfast trays. Well, she knew one thing. The cat liked eggs.

"Looks like the cat has your breakfast," she informed Gus as she eased off his lap.

"The devil you say!" The outraged man scrambled out of his chair and stomped over to where the cat was, still eating without showing any alarm. Instead of removing the cat from the cabinet and its impromptu meal, Gus stared at it. "I think he's eating *your* breakfast. After all, he's your cat."

It was a valid point, but as much as she wanted a pet to call her own, she wasn't the type of owner who'd share her meals with her pet. At the very least, she'd get first pick of the food. At the beginning of their relationship, Gus was fairly easy to boss around, but not so much now. In fact, he was starting to push back and on occasion, kick up a fuss. Although she'd never tell him, she kind of liked it. It didn't mean she would roll over and give in. "I can't believe you'd allow your sweetheart to starve."

He threw a disbelieving look over his shoulder and picked up the untouched tray. "Knowing you, you'll figure out some way to get a second breakfast. If not, I'm willing to share my breakfast with you. If you do a good job making up with Herman, we might get him to take us to the Chinese buffet, which would make up for a meager breakfast.

It sounded tempting—possibly enough to eat crow.

Chapter Nine

EUNICE'S FEET SLOWED as she approached Herman's room. Even though she knew what she had to do, it didn't make it any easier. Aware of her reluctance, Gus had his arm hooked through hers as if afraid she might bolt.

Two of the ladies who normally played bingo giggled as they passed by the two of them in the corridor. Their laughter set Eunice's teeth on edge. She stumbled to a halt and inhaled deeply. *No one* laughed at her. She wanted to give those old biddies a piece of her mind, but they vanished down the hall before she could come up with something more cutting than implying they cheated at bingo, since most of the residents did.

"Come on," Gus urged while jiggling her arm. "Don't get cold feet now. We're almost there."

As if she needed the reminder. What she wouldn't give for a distraction. Her eyes scanned the corridor. Even the sudden appearance of the activity director with a request for Eunice to chair yet another committee would be welcome. No activity director in sight but someone even better. Marci, the senior sleuths' mentor, was headed their way with the use of a three-prong cane. Normally, the woman used a wheelchair, but the physical therapist must have insisted she try to walk more to strengthen her leg.

Her stride was a little rough, but it was a vast improvement over the recovering detective's former method of getting around, which varied from rolling down the hallway or furniture surfing in her unit. Marci saw them and held up her hand. "Oh good. I'm trying to round up the sleuths for an informal meeting in Herman's room."

"Herman's room?" Eunice queried, knowing his room was no bigger than Marci's. It made her wonder how he rated above the rest of us.

"Yes." Marci nodded and gestured in the direction of the room. "With any luck, Jake and Lola will already be there. I was surprised to see you. I was told..." She coughed, cutting off whatever could have followed.

The implication hung in the air. What had she heard? Gus beat her to a denial.

"What you heard isn't the truth. Eunice is no fast gal."

What! Eunice delivered a sharp slap to his arm. Hopefully, it would be enough to discourage any more remarks.

Her sweetheart shot her a puzzled look, but it didn't slow down his tongue. "Most people have the wrong idea about Eunice and my midnight antics. What we were really doing was—"

She gave two sharp raps to his arm since one hadn't done the trick. The man would probably tell everyone all he knew about the newest furry resident. In no time, the cat would be history. He dropped her arm and stepped away, rubbing the abused limb that had reddened due to the abuse.

"That hurt," he said with a bit of a whine in his tone. "You didn't have to beat on me as if whipping a stubborn mule."

"Yes," Marci agreed. "That's certainly not the way to maintain a relationship."

The comment carried a touch of judgment to Eunice's ears. It made her want to defend herself, but that would mean revealing her secret pet. Even though it almost made her choke, she managed to say, "You're right." She turned and nodded at Gus. "I'm sorry. I just want what happened between the two of us to remain private."

Marci held up her hand as amusement danced over her face. "Say no more. Look. Jake and Lola are here."

They turned to see the rest of the senior sleuths sauntering down the hallway. Herman pushed his door open and gave the corridor a suspicious survey. Finding no one with the exception of the sleuths, he gestured for them to come in. "Hurry. The last thing I need is that chatty aide to see you all piling into my room. It took forever to convince her that it wasn't me barking behind Lola's door. I have doubts that she bought my excuse." He pulled in Gus, who made the mistake of lingering in the open passageway, and gave the door a firm slam.

Even though she was supposed to play nice and make her apologies to Herman, the way he manhandled her sweetie caused her to narrow her eyes and momentarily contemplate an act of satisfying revenge. *No, I can't do that. I'm a pet owner now.* Instead, she exhaled loudly. "I'm sure your slamming the door should keep everything low-key."

A panicked look crossed Herman's face. He held his finger to his lips and silently opened the door to peer outside. After a few seconds, Herman pulled in his head, then shut the door quietly and leaned against it with a relieved sigh. "No one at the station. I heard there was free cake and ice cream in the lounge for someone's birthday. They all must be there."

A general discussion about the desirability of cake over pie broke out as Marci eased herself down into a chair. She allowed it to go on long past cake winning the debate. Lola insisted that Boston Cream Pie was both cake *and* pie, which started the argument again. A metallic clatter stopped the conversation, and all eyes went to Marci, who held her metal cane over a filing cabinet with the possibility of another tapping.

"No more," Herman begged while holding up his hands in entreaty. His ability to do that was a feat in such tight quarters.

His request caused Marci to grin and lower her cane. "Let's get this over with. As you know, Lance and I are trying to keep ourselves out of the loop, which explains why we are meeting in Herman's room as opposed to my own spacious suite."

Eunice chuckled along with a few other sleuths, knowing that all the rooms in the center were far from spacious. The only reason Marci's unit had slightly more room was that she hadn't left her actual home and did not bring all her treasures with her as the other residents had. The good detective had hopes of leaving eventually, once healed, and returning to her job.

When the laughter died down, Marci continued. "As you remember, Lance explained that not much was found when they tried to track down Loretta. She left, taking her car with her and apparently mailing a letter on her way out of town. I believe Jake raised a question of a paper trail?"

"Paper trail?" Eunice asked. "That's news to me." She elbowed Gus. "Did you hear anything about it?"

"Ah…" Gus hesitated and stared at a corner of the ceiling. "Well, about that…" He tried to reach for Eunice's hand, which she pulled

LATE FOR SQUARE DANCING

away with a sniff.

"Go on. I have the feeling I won't like what you have to say. Might as well get it out. Treat it like a band-aid."

"Geesh," Gus muttered. "That makes it worse. I hate band-aids. Well, ah, we had an impromptu meeting when we came back from our outing to the neighborhood."

Her mouth dropped open. Here she thought she had come so far. It was no secret, in the beginning, no one was too fond of her. The only reason they had tolerated her was her constant threat to inform the administration of their sneaking out of the center. Maybe it wasn't the best way to make friends, but it did bring her into the Senior Sleuths, if only to keep her mum on their activities. She thought once they'd witnessed her deductive skills, they'd be fans. Up to this point, not so much, as far as she could tell.

While she had shown her expertise in things such as furniture from her work in home furnishings, Eunice had also demonstrated the fine art of getting out of sticky situations by using people's unflattering stereotype of the elderly as dim-witted and confused. Most people would sit around pouting about it. Instead, she chose to use it to her advantage. "Did you find a trail?"

Jake nodded at the words. "Yeah. That's why we're all here."

The sleuths all turned their attention to Marci. She cleared her throat and gestured to them. "I could have told you individually, but felt it was better to do it as a group. However, there really isn't much to say. There was no paper trail. The first time they searched for Loretta, they naturally monitored her credit or bank cards for use with no luck. Nothing has happened since that time."

A moan and a smattering of dismayed expressions filled the room. What had started as a simple search for a disenchanted wife showed all the signs of remaining an unsolved cold case. Not too surprising. Since he requested the information about the paper trail, Jake was the first to speak. "What should we deduce from this?"

"Cash," Lola offered. "Loretta used cash. Folks who don't want to be found often use folding money only." The woman pushed back in the only decent chair in the room and gave a slow, confident smile.

Thunderation. Eunice gave herself an all over shake. Maybe she *had* been off her game, trying to find and hide her kitty. Lola got the jump on her. She inhaled deeply and tried to think of what else could help find the elusive Loretta. "I'd expect such a response from you with your association with criminal types and all."

Herman pushed to his feet and raised his voice. "Excuse me! You don't talk to Lola that way. Take it back!"

Eunice sucked in her lips and covered her mouth with her hands. Good heavens! How did that slip out? Here she was trying to be on her good behavior, too. No way Herman would drive her around now. Her shoulders slumped forward as she realized her razor tongue had got her into trouble again. Rescue came from the most unexpected place.

Lola chuckled. "Herman, don't take on so. Everyone knows Vegas is associated with the Mafia. It is what it is. I still stand by my statement that money is the best way to hide your path."

"True…" Eunice found herself agreeing and hoped it might serve as a type of olive branch. "Money is good until it runs out. Since she has been gone for a while, she'll need more of it. I suspect there's no sugar daddy waiting on her, which means she'll have to work somewhere." Her fingers interlaced as she contemplated how they could find where the mysterious Loretta was working. "I imagine she'd do something that either she'd be paid for in cash or some job where she got a bunch of tips."

"Good idea," Marci said and clapped her hands together. "Nothing has been found using her legal name, Loretta Jane Simmons."

That made sense. Eunice found herself nodding to herself. Using one's legal name would be the same as putting a neon arrow pointing to the individual. Most of the mysteries and crime dramas featured characters who used part of their names or even their maiden names. "I got it. Check for her maiden name or names similar to it. Also…" Eunice held up a finger as she remembered the plot to an old mystery. "…check for questionable jobs. The ones that don't ask for references or a social security number."

After relating the information, Eunice's shoulder went back, and she puffed out her meager chest. Maybe she was a Johnny-come-lately today, but her deductions might be the secret to locating the missing Loretta.

Jake's hand went up. It wasn't uncommon for some of the sleuths to raise their hands to speak. It just showed how ingrained the gesture was. Marci acknowledged him with a hand gesture. "Go ahead."

Jake made sure to meet everyone's eyes before speaking. "I know I asked for the paper trail, but I'm beginning to think Loretta is dead. Maybe we should be concentrating on her husband, Robert."

Thanks, Jake, for stealing my glory, Eunice thought to herself.

"If that's the case," Marci began in a solemn tone, "we must leave it to the police. Our job was only to investigate the possible whereabouts of Loretta. That also means Robert is much more devious than Lance suspected. Fairly gutsy to ask your neighbor detective to look into the disappearance of your wife, knowing you murdered her." The beleaguered detective gave a derisive snort. She held up her hands. "Looks like you're all off the case."

Chapter Ten

ONCE MARCI ANNOUNCED there was no reason to pursue the search, the room emptied as if someone had shouted *fire*. Even the good detective picked up her cane and was on her way. Only Gus, Eunice, and Herman remained. Since it was Herman's room, his presence was understandable. The man propped both hands on his hips and arched a shaggy eyebrow. "You two. Waiting for something? Everyone else has hit the road."

"Yep," Gus agreed, then shrugged. He shoved both hands into his pockets. "Not sure why Jake said something and everyone thinks it's a done deal. Yesterday, he was trying to follow a paper trail and today Loretta's dead. Peculiar."

A kitchen chair bumped across the floor as Herman shoved it into place at the table. To prove he was listening despite his tidying, he gave a grunt. "I noticed that, too. It even appeared like Marci was in a hurry to shut us down. Makes you think."

In most cases, Herman was not Eunice's champion. It almost sounded like he was more a fan of *her* theory, rather than Jake's dead Loretta one. "Yeah. I didn't even consider the possibility of Loretta working a cash-only job or working under another name."

Both men turned and stared as if they had forgotten Eunice was in the room. Their actions emboldened her. One thing she had learned in the furniture business was when you had someone's attention, you ran with it. While she might not be trying to sell a couch, she still had some solid possibilities about the case. "She might have even bought a fake ID. They come up with social security numbers of dead people. Dead folks don't complain about identity theft. Heard you can get one for fifty dollars. I imagine those are beer cards with the photo looking nothing like the person who bought it. Of course, the more you pay the better they are, I imagine. I don't know Loretta's plans, but if she was thinking of accusing her husband of killing her, she would have had another identity already planned."

"Possible," Herman admitted as he pushed a second chair up to the table. "Could have been an impulsive thing, too. Maybe the two of them had an argument about going on vacation or something. Loretta's husband disagrees and doesn't want to go to some all-inclusive resort she picked out. Maybe he doesn't like to travel or balks because it cost too much. Whatever it is sends Loretta off into a tizzy. She decides to make him pay for his attitude."

Instead of participating in the conversation, Gus wandered over to Herman's desk and picked up a coin that was lying on the surface. He held it up and squinted at it. "Is this one of those valuable coins from our last case?"

Herman stopped moving chairs around to reply. "Would I leave it on the desk for you to pick up if it were?"

Either Gus mistook the question for being rhetorical or he just didn't hear because he didn't answer. The thing with Gus was you never knew which one it was. He might be using his perceived disability to opt out of conversations whenever he felt like it. Eunice allowed his silence on more than one occasion, not wanting to go through a long story again that he may or may not want to hear.

Just when she had given up on a reply, Gus turned and pointed to Herman. "You sure you've never been married? That scenario sounded like a man with experience living with an angry woman."

The possibility intrigued Eunice. Most folks have a secret or two. Some of them weren't worth hearing about, such as forgetting the words to the Star-Spangled Banner in second grade while soloing in the class play. Others could have done jail time or even disappeared like Loretta. Forgetting to mention a spouse, even a former one, was kind of a big deal in a community that thrived on gossip. It was the kind of tidbit that would make her welcome in all the various groups that had previously shunned her. If she had an antenna, it would have gone up as she strained to hear Herman's reply.

"You don't have to be married to be around irritated females. I've known a few in my life." He said the line in a matter-of-fact way. Probably the same way someone else would have admitted to having camped or fished at some time in their lives.

Unless he met those particular females in traffic, Eunice suspected there must have been an intimate relationship in the man's past. It made her want to know more, but present circumstance being what they were, she'd have to curb her curiosity at least until they got back from the store.

Her sweetie returned to her side, having abandoned the desk and whatever treasures resided there. Gus placed his hand under her elbow and gave it an affectionate squeeze. There might be hope for the man yet.

"Honey? Isn't there something you want to ask Herman?"

Drat. The elbow squeeze was not a flirty gesture at all. Just like him to nag her about an unpleasant duty. She swallowed hard and steeled herself for the deed. Kitty had to eat and using a box of torn celebrity gossip magazines in place of litter wasn't cutting it. "Um…" She stalled, not liking the feel of *sorry* in her mouth. "I'm amazed at how good you look in that blue plaid shirt. It really brings out the blue in your eyes. Personally, I thought you were more of an autumn colors guy, but the blue works for you."

"Eunice…" Gus raised his voice a tiny bit. Since his hand had slipped from Eunice's elbow, he went to grab it again, but she jerked it away.

"Stop it!" She glared at her sweetie. "I know what I am doing." She turned to face Herman. This must be how the soldiers felt when hitting Omaha Beach. Well, probably not exactly since they knew they were going to be shot at and possibly killed. As far as she knew, Herman didn't have a gun. Weapons weren't allowed in the facility, but neither was liquor, cigars, or animals. Residents had sneaked in all of them at one time or another. It wasn't like the administration would kick them out. However, a gun might be a different matter.

No holster bulge, so she was probably safe. "I shouldn't have said what I did about you being a square dance expert, and I am willing to help you with the committee."

Saying the words so quickly, Eunice didn't have time for a breath, which left her gasping air and waiting for a response.

Silence. Herman reached for his handlebar mustache he was so proud of and tweaked the ends. "I'm not sure I got what you said. Could you repeat it?"

Oh, he knew what she said. A person could bet on it. It wouldn't surprise her if the man wasn't enjoying her discomfort. She knew it wouldn't be easy. She turned back toward Gus, who shrugged his shoulders. No help there.

"I said," she started, making sure to talk louder and enunciating each word carefully, "I was sorry about throwing you under the bus when it came to square dancing. I'd be glad to help."

Even though Herman didn't have a hearing issue he would admit to, he cupped his ear. "Did you say *takeover* the square-dancing committee?"

She hadn't said that. Obviously, it was what it would take to get on Herman's good side. "Okay. I'll do it."

"Great!" Herman said, then grabbed her arm and towed her to the door. "We're going to see the activity director and tell her what you just told me, except maybe not the sorry part. I'm not taking a chance on your changing your mind."

"Whatever," she murmured to herself, a comment she had heard more than one employee use, and it fit the situation. Because of Herman's height, she had to take two steps to his one. "Slow down, Jolly Plaid Giant. I can't keep up."

Herman did slow as they neared the activity director's office. The door stood ajar and the woman was in. *Joy.* They stood outside the door, unsure if knocking was appropriate if the door was already open. The dilemma was solved by the director asking them to come in, which they did.

Herman nudged her as if she had forgotten why they were there. What was it with the male population today? They all seemed to be nag, nag, along with dragging her to places she didn't want to go. "I'm here to replace Herman on the square dance thingy. He's not really that good at square dancing, dancing in general, organizing things, or—"

"Enough!" Herman interrupted. "She's taking over for me on the committee."

Had he said *committee* before? Maybe he had. She couldn't remember. An uneasy feeling washed over her. Her nostrils flared as her breathing became more rapid. Everyone knew Eunice could get things done on her own. However, committees involved other people. Individuals who talked everything to death and slowed the whole process down. Even worse, they might think their ideas were better, which was totally ridiculous. People made things so much harder to get things done. Surely, she could pick her own people who she'd forget to invite to meetings.

"Wonderful!" the director enthused. "I can't wait to tell Pearl and Carmen. They're itching to get started."

Pearl and Carmen? Pearl gossiped more than she did. Carmen cheated at bingo. It sounded like a door slamming shut, locking her in what had to be purgatory.

Chapter Eleven

NSIDE THE CENTER'S dining room, there was the scent of roasting chicken along with pans clattering and a loud discussion among the kitchen help concerning the fridge inventory. The limited amount of eggs and butter would determine the evening dessert. Eunice rubbed her eyes as she wished away the possibility of Jell-O for two nights in a row.

Maybe the dining room wasn't the quietest place, but there was no way Eunice was inviting Pearl and Carmen to her room that contained a kitten. Besides, the women might also take it as a friendly gesture. That wasn't something she wanted to convey.

Eunice tapped her pen against the table, not knowing where to lead her troupe of two. Even though no one discussed it, she naturally assumed leadership. It was a given. All she had to do was get her minions into place. However, help might be nice. "Okay. Let's start the meeting."

Both minions gave her a startled look, but Pearl gave a slow shake of her gray dusted hair. "Not sure what you're doing. You're acting like you're in charge and all. I know I wasn't told that you were the big boss. Carmen and I were a committee before you came along. You're a Johnny-come-lately as far as I can tell." She turned to address the other woman at the table. "Carmen, what do you think?"

"A dance," Carmen announced, with bright eyes and a hopeful

smile, somehow missing the entire question. "It's been over a year since our last dance. We need another." She swayed in her chair and wrapped her arms gently around herself as if slow dancing. "It would be so nice."

It was obvious the woman was mimicking slow dancing and not square dancing. Eunice was ready to point out her error when Pearl interrupted.

"That sounds like a plan. A good one. People need a reason to take dance lessons. If they knew an event was coming up, they'd readily do it. Not all of them, of course, but enough to make the project worthwhile. I motion we have a dance. Any seconds?"

"Second," Carmen announced while raising her hand.

In lieu of a gavel, Pearl smacked the table with her hand. "Motion carried. Now, let's examine our most immediate concern— dance lessons. Our best bet would be morning lessons. That way it doesn't interfere with bingo, scrapbooking, or the poodle visits, which are all in the afternoon. An afternoon class would give people reasons not to come. Most of the men like to nap after their lunch meal."

Good gracious! Pearl was railroading this thing. *No one* ran over Eunice. She put up her hand, mimicking Carmen's earlier action. Maybe it was appropriate behavior in a committee. "Ah, wait a minute."

Pearl turned her head slowly toward Eunice. The action was reminiscent of animatronics at a theme park. Right about then, her mouth would creak open and some prerecorded message would play. Musing on Pearl's similarity to a robot caused her to be surprised when acknowledged.

"Would you like to add something? Does the idea of morning dance lessons not appeal to you? I wouldn't be surprised considering the late hours you and Gus keep. No worries, I'm sure we will have plenty of participants without you two." She added a dismissive sniff that caused Carmen to chuckle.

Now they were making fun of her. No one did that and lived to talk about it. Since she wasn't planning on killing anyone, she was forced to modify her thought a little. There was no way she'd let Steamroller Pearl and Cheating Carmen get the better of her. Eunice knew she had a reputation as a cantankerous woman, but she was also the same female who got things done. If there was going to be a dance, by George she'd be in charge. Not only to knock Pearl off her high horse but also to show Gus she was more efficient than his deceased wife and could dance circles around everyone, which was fitting since sometimes circles were used in square dancing.

"I was going to say the morning was a perfect time. Since I'm an early bird, I'll be sure to be there with my *boyfriend*." She made a point of emphasizing the last word since neither Pearl nor Carmen had a gentleman friend. Men weren't thick on the ground at the center, either. There was a good chance the women would have to be each other's partner. It was also hard to get the few men who were at the center to actually participate in the events. Most of them must have decided early on that they would not interact with the other residents. A few like Jake did, though.

"Oh." Pearl's penciled in eyebrows arched. "Good," she added, although her sullen expression said otherwise. "Morning lessons, do I hear a second?"

Her minion, Carmen, would second the action, but Eunice was

tired of being left out, which is why she loudly announced, "Second."

Both Pearl and Carmen shot each other baffled looks, then turned to stare at Eunice, who smiled sweetly. The first rule of dealing with other people, especially the sneaky sort, was to keep them guessing.

"All right, then," Pearl continued as if she hadn't just been surprised. "I guess we can adjourn the meeting. Carmen can put the notification of dance lessons in the newsletter and send it out today. I'll check with the activity director to see the exact day the lessons will start."

Carmen gave a little salute, then pushed up from her chair.

"Don't go running off," Eunice said in a breathless fashion. Her attempt to grab some power and push Carmen from her Boss of Everything failed. She needed more drastic measures. "We haven't even decided where the dance will be."

"Right here," Pearl gestured to the dining room with its wooden tables and plastic potted palms. We'll have it after supper, of course."

Eunice made sure to mimic Pearl's gesture. "Here?" She raised her voice. "You must be kidding."

Once again, the two women exchanged glances before speaking. Carmen cleared her throat, demonstrating she wasn't the best at public speaking. "We had the last dance here."

"True." Eunice nodded her head and gave Carmen an approving glance, equivalent to a head pat. "If you remember, that was mostly slow dances where couples hugged and swayed."

"I know," Carmen gushed with a dreamy look. "I loved it."

Apparently, she had. It made Eunice wonder what resident the woman had her eye on. "Square dancing is much more vigorous and requires a lot of room like in a…" She paused as she tried to think of anywhere in the center that had more room. Nothing came to mind since most areas were crowded with furniture. An idea did blossom. The perfect way to assume control. "We need a barn. Hay bales. A platform for the caller. So much more room than this tiny dining room offers."

Not sold on the idea at all, Pearl narrowed her eyes and shook her head. "Barns are dirty. They have animals in them, for Pete's sake. How would we get to your mythical barn?"

The fact she called it *mythical* meant Eunice was getting under her skin. She made an airy gesture with her hand as if waving away any concern. "Oh, it's not a *barn* barn. Oh, no. It's one of those things they use for wedding venues. Everyone wants to have their reception or square dances in a barn."

Carmen clapped her hands together in glee. "Oh, yes! My grandniece just got married in one. There was all this exposed wood, but they had nice touches to fancy it up. It even had chandeliers and white lace tablecloths. Do you know where we could rent such a place?"

"No worries." Eunice placed her hand over her heart. "I have a friend who owes me a favor."

She ignored Pearl's disbelieving glare, stood, and moved to hook arms with Carmen. "Let's go find the activity director and tell her we're going to have a *barn* dance."

Chapter Twelve

A SMUG SMILE graced Eunice's features, and there was a bounce in her step as she exited the dining room triumphantly. That Pearl thought she had control of the committee. A chuckle escaped as she considered the expression on the women's faces when she pointed out that pushing back the tables and chairs in the dining room would simply not serve. Obviously, Pearl knew nothing about how to motivate people. Pearl was a real dragon lady. She thought she could throw her weight around and get her way. It probably worked most of the time, but she had failed to count on Eunice's tenacity. No one would steamroll her. News this good had to be shared.

Other residents strolled by. One or two nodded in her direction. A man she had scolded for yelling *bingo* when he didn't have a winning card made a wide berth around her. Well, he should. Who knows what other cons the man might try to pull?

Before she got pulled into committee planning, the sleuths had met to discuss the latest case. Marci pretty much told them to forget about it. The average person would follow her advice, but she was far from average. In fact, the instructions to stop made her want to try that much harder to demonstrate how creative and clever old folks could be.

What she needed was to round up a few sleuths. After all, when she pinpointed where the missing Loretta was, it would be good to have witnesses who could relate her detailed deductions to both Lance and Marci.

Ahead, she recognized the bald pate of her sweetie and the man was moving fast. "Gus!"

No response. Maybe the man really was hard of hearing. She picked up her gait to catch up. "Gus! I know you heard me."

Nothing. As she drew closer, she grabbed his arm, which caused him to stumble, but he regained his balance and shot her a furious look. "Are you trying to kill me? I thought for a moment it was the cold, bony hand of death reaching for me."

"Ha." Sometimes Gus's sense of humor was entirely lacking. "My hand isn't bony." She glanced down at her thin hand wrapped around Gus's arm. "Not too much. Anyhow, where are you going in such a hurry?"

Her sweetie turned his head to peer over his shoulder. Then he put a finger up to his lips. "Be quiet. It's a secret. You can come with me. We're meeting in Lola's room."

Why would they be meeting in Lola's room? It could be she managed to convince Lance to allow her a little extra cuddle time with the tiny dog, Bear. Most of the residents enjoyed petting an animal. Many had stuffed animals they enjoyed holding and stroking. Since she had a cat in her room, the possibility didn't tempt her. "I'm not sure if I want to see the dog. It's cute and all, but I have things to do. There's my own furry friend. There's also the issue of finding a reasonably clean barn for a hoedown."

Gus's brow furrowed, and he wrinkled his nose. "Excuse me. You said something about a barn?"

It would be hard to explain without looking foolish. It *had* felt inspired at the time. Now, not so much, and she wondered if her tendency to want to one-up other people may not have served her well. "It's a long story. Later, when no one is around, I'll explain."

"You're not interested in finding Loretta?" Gus asked with a wink.

"Of course, I am. Why didn't you say so before?"

He placed his index finger up to his lips.

Oh yeah, it was supposed to be a secret. Apparently, they were going behind Marci's back. It shocked her. Now *she* was ready to continue the search, and she expected the others to obey. Who knew they were rebels among the tame sheep residents of Greener Pastures? It gave her hope. She nodded, willing to keep her mouth shut.

It didn't take long to reach Lola's room. Herman opened the door and ushered them in quickly. He asked, "Did anyone see you?"

Good Heavens. Were they in a spy movie? Eunice shook her head at the absurdity of the man's action. "Of course, they saw us. Unless they were blind. However, I'm not sure if they thought about it overly much. What does it matter? The only person you're trying to deceive is Marci, who wasn't in the corridors. I'd say we're safe."

Herman glanced at Gus, who shrugged. "What she said."

Across the room, Lola sat at a small desk bathed in the light of a laptop screen. She glanced at the newest entries. "I'm glad you are here. I could use your combined wits to decide what names our Loretta might have used. I have a site that allows you to research names for a modest fee. It's not a hundred percent accurate or up to date, but it might be a starting point."

No one had to tell Eunice twice. Leaving her sweetie behind, she hustled over to the computer. Eunice grabbed a nearby folding chair and pulled it up to the desk, bumping into Lola. "Oops."

The woman gave a heavy sigh. "It's not exactly easy to type with these acrylic nails. I had just typed in *Simmons*. You just bumped my elbow, messing it all up."

"Oh." Eunice's eyebrows shot up. "Sorry. I can help. I used to be a pretty good typist. They used to call me ol' speedy fingers." She held up the digits in question and wiggled them. "Look, no annoying long nails. Here." She moved her chair closer, crowding Lola. "Let me."

"Like I have a choice," Lola complained as she stood. "Her name is Loretta Jane Simmons."

"Yes, I know." Eunice's fingers flew across the keys as she typed the first name. Murmured conversation amongst the three caused her to stop to listen. Not wanting to be too obvious, she pretended to be stymied. "How do you spell Jane?"

The three stopped talking and Herman answered. "The usual."

Well, that was no help. "Is it J-A-N-E or -A-Y-N-E?"

"Who spells Jane with a Y?" Herman asked with a smirk. He acted like it was the most ridiculous thing he'd ever heard. His attitude chafed a little, causing Eunice to bristle. "Plenty of people spell it that way. Move into the twenty-first century."

The zinger shut the man's mouth for a minute. It would do him good to realize he wasn't the know-it-all he thought he was. A loud throat-clearing forced Eunice to look away from the computer only to discover Herman had moved closer.

Noticing her attention, he said, "You know, Loretta wasn't born in the twenty-first century. I doubt she'd be using a new-fangled spelling."

He had a point, but she wasn't ready to concede it, though. "Maybe. Could be she's trying to start over with a new name. Folks often use parts of their names when creating a new identity. It's as if they can't let that part of themselves go, and it's usually their undoing because that's often how they are traced. Loretta Jane Simmons could become Lori or Rita. Instead of Simmons, she might go for Jayne with the Y, which might make it sound more like a last name. We should try all the different variations of the name."

"Makes sense," Lola agreed from the other side.

Of course, it did. Eunice typed the final letters of the name, then hit the *search* button. A small icon of a bloodhound appeared while a small text block appeared above it with the information that it had located twenty-six people with that name. "Wouldn't have thought it was that common of a name."

Herman's shadow enveloped her as he peered over her shoulder and pointed at some names. "Can't be that one. Says she's ninety-one." He pointed to another one. "Not that one, either. Lives in Texas. I suspect that would be too far for Loretta to drive."

The overpowering aroma of Herman's cologne, along with the scent of the butterscotch he was nursing, invaded the area, causing Eunice to put up her hands. "Back up. I need my personal space. I can print these out, and we can all look at them without anyone sitting in my lap."

Each Loretta had several names underneath hers along with an age and address. There was a button to click on for more information. Eunice clicked on it and a pop-up announced that it needed

$19.99 to proceed. "Hey, I need someone's credit card to finish this."

No answer. "Did you hear me? A mere $19.99 is the only thing standing between us locating Loretta and showing everyone that the Senior Sleuths still have it."

Instead, everyone was looking at one another or the ceiling. Anywhere but at Eunice. She snorted. "Well, I didn't bring my purse. Are you all going to give up like Jake did over twenty bucks?"

Herman snorted. "Not sure he gave up. I wouldn't be surprised if he isn't holed up in his own room scrolling through names on his own laptop. The man I know wouldn't have given up that fast. It could be he just didn't want to upset Marci, and that's why he agreed that the case was done."

A spy might pretend to do something else to throw folks off the trail as he worked to solve the case, and rumors ran rampant through the center. One was that Jake had played a spy in the war years. It was probably a made-up story. It wouldn't be too surprising if Jake had made it up himself. Still, she exhaled audibly. Why was the world so filled with competition? All it meant was she had to get a jump on Jake now. It just wasn't the police she was trying to impress and outdistance. "I need a credit card. Now!"

With some general grumbling, both the men pulled out their wallets. Gus opened his and announced, "I was robbed! No driver's license. No credit cards. There's no real money to speak of." Herman gave the man a disbelieving stare as he plucked his own card out of his wallet and handed it to Eunice.

Not willing to take a chance on his changing his mind, Eunice took the card and typed in the number. There was an image of a door opening. A paragraph of text appeared describing a Loretta

Jane, who married a man named Harold back in 1943. They had three children named Darlene, Donald, and Madeline. Loretta had a driver's license. Her parents were Norman and Orillia. In her life, she had moved five times, and it listed all five addresses.

A snort sounded behind her. She didn't have to turn to know it was Herman. The man hadn't backed off even after being told to. Could be he wanted to see how his money was being spent.

"Eunice," he grumbled, making the name sound like a complaint. "You clicked on the wrong woman. She's seventy-six and married to the wrong man."

"It's hard to think straight when you're in my personal bubble, sucking up all the air. If that isn't enough, you're a smell factory with your cologne and candy. It's not surprising I picked the wrong woman. Obviously, we need to try again. You pick next."

Her suggestion seemed to mollify the man, who ran his finger a scant inch above the screen. He stopped and tapped on one name. Eunice clicked on the chosen Loretta. "Let's hope this one's the right one."

"It is," Herman confirmed. "There's even a Robert Simmons associated with her."

She didn't like the sound of this. What if Herman was right? Boy, she'd never hear the end of it. Then again, if he hadn't overloaded her olfactory gland, she might have been able to think straight and would have clicked on the right name to begin with. She shifted in her chair and cut her eyes only to discover everyone's attention was trained on her, waiting for her to make the click. Her gut told her this was probably the right Loretta, but it might not yield any helpful information.

A warning came up about paying another $19.99, but Eunice

typed in Herman's card numbers without asking. He was the one who picked the nice candidate. It was fitting he paid.

"Not again," Herman said.

"Searches are never without cost." Eunice enlarged the screen results to three hundred percent to avoid Herman crowding her again. The bloodhound icon was back, along with the results. It was their very own Loretta Jane Simmons. She was still listed as being married to Robert and had apparently not been declared dead. Her most recent address was where Robert still resided and down the street from Lance. No children. She had a brother named Keith, though.

"Looks like she was married before. The husband's name is Jonas Hogg. That's a start."

She didn't really think it was but felt if she said so she'd be as big a killjoy as Jake—even if the man *was* working another angle. Loretta must have divorced the man, possibly tired of being referred to as Mrs. Hogg. On the screen, there was another pop-up that offered to show more information such as criminal records. Without asking, Eunice clicked on it. Luckily, she didn't have to put in the credit card information again. It could be that Loretta had a criminal past. If so, she might return to her life of crime to support herself. Not only would she be locating a missing person and taking the focus off Robert, but she'd also be bringing in a criminal, just like a regular cop.

On the screen, the image of a door swung open again displaying no criminal record of any kind. However, their Loretta did have a nail-tech license along with a CDL license. That was something. She made sure to print the latest record.

"Our girl could be doing nails somewhere or driving a truck."

"That narrows it down," Lola joked. "There are nail salons on every corner and plenty of truck drivers. Move on over. I want to put my name in and see what I get. It will give us a chance to see how well this site works."

There might not be anything more to get on Loretta, but Eunice moved only a few inches. She refused to miss out on what the site might have on Lola. She watched as the only other female sleuth typed out her first name M-A-R-Y. "I can't believe you can't spell your own name."

The comment caused the typist to chuckle. "Mary isn't a show-girl name. It would be hard to be taken seriously with the name Mary. Let's see what we get."

By this time, the cute bloodhound who was searching for clues was getting a bit annoying. A block of information came up, but Lola changed the font back to normal size, making it hard to read, but not before Eunice noticed the age. Two years older than the woman would admit. She expected as much since most of the women at the center tended to move their birthdate forward. It wasn't exactly a crime.

Lola pursed her lips, then shook her head. "Not sure how much faith I'd put in this site. It has me married to my brother, Andrew."

"Go on," Eunice said with a smirk. "Check out your sordid criminal past."

"Not on my dime, or I should say, $19.99," Herman asserted and picked up his credit card. "It's hard to know what to do next with these kinds of results."

The prospect of visiting nail salons in the surrounding counties didn't appeal either. "Maybe we should try different names, such as her maiden name," Gus suggested. Leave it to her honey to come with an excellent suggestion.

"Let's do that." She seconded his idea and cut her eyes to Herman, who folded his arms and shook his head. Sure, she could use her own credit card, but the bill would go directly to her daughter, who managed her money, which would raise a red flag for sure. No doubt her offspring would be calling the center; certain her mother was being suckered into some Internet con. With her luck, she'd be banned from using all computers. No, thank you.

She accepted there would be no more financial help coming from Herman. It made her remember that her goal today was to get to the store and buy some supplies for her kitty. A small charge at a drugstore or convenience store wouldn't raise any eyebrows. Her daughter would erroneously assume she boarded the center bus with the other mobile seniors for a shopping trip to the local mall. It was partially the truth since she was going shopping and would be with other seniors.

"We should go back to the neighborhood." She half-turned to glance at Lola. "Didn't you need something from the store? We could stop on our way back."

Her brilliance amazed her. Herman could refuse Lola nothing.

Chapter Thirteen

THE CLATTER OF typewriter keys, then a pause followed by a muttered curse, had Eunice cutting her eyes to Gus as they both hovered over Jake while he glared at the labels curled around the typewriter cylinder. "Stupid thing. It keeps typing the wrong letter. At this pace, we'll never get this done. Whose idea was this?"

At first, they weren't going to include Jake in their information-gathering mission since he thought Loretta was dead and said as much. After considering how upset he might be at being excluded, they decided otherwise. Actually, Gus was the one who had pushed the point since he and Jake had been friends forever. Personally, Eunice felt leaving him behind would serve the man well. Her thinking might have something to do with her lack of friends, too. With a deep inhale, she filed the thought for deeper introspection later.

Lola, who was behind Eunice said, "It was mine."

The door creaked open as Katie, the actual owner of the office and Jake's niece, entered. Lola lowered her voice to a whisper as she continued, "You can't just go up to a house without a reason, especially the home of a possible murderer."

"Agreed," Jake admitted with a nod. He glanced back to judge how close Katie was, gave a friendly wave, then continued. "Still, you think trotting over with junk mail with mailing labels on it for

Loretta will do the trick? Who does that type of thing?"

"Nice people, good neighbors," Eunice was quick to point out. It was the only workable solution they had come up with so far. Since they had already descended on the neighborhood as church missionaries, a cosmetic saleswoman, and one confused motorist, they had used up the good covers. It wouldn't work for them all to show up at the door together as if several decades too late for trick or treating. They'd agree a couple would work best. In the interest of getting the most pertinent facts, Eunice volunteered herself and Jake.

It was hard to say who was more surprised, Jake or Gus. Her excuse for picking Jake was he was already suspicious of the husband and would be more likely to notice anything off. No need to point out that Gus might not hear exactly what was said. She couldn't chance Herman, either. She needed the man's goodwill if she was going to make it to the store. No need to mess things up by trying to work *with* the man. If he said the wrong thing and fouled up their scheme, she might end up pointing it out. Jake was a former pilot, rumored to be a possible spy, and might be the better candidate. His response to the rumors was all pilots in the war were spies since they had the opportunity to see more from up high.

"Uncle Jake," Katie called out from her desk across the room. "I'd be glad to type out those labels on the computer for you. It would take no time using the printer."

That was what they didn't need. Someone else in the know. Helpful people could be hard to discourage, especially one as sweet as Jake's niece. Still, they didn't need anyone to know what they were up to. Eunice sucked in her lips, wondering how Jake might respond.

His shoulders went up as he barked. "I can do it myself! I know no one thinks I can do it, but I can."

"Sorry, Uncle Jake. Just trying to help," Katie answered, with the tiniest bit of chagrin lingering in her tone. "I didn't mean to upset you."

Jake sighed and spun the rolling chair around to face his niece. The senior sleuths moved out of the way like a curtain parting to allow the two good eye contact as they spoke.

"Back when I was in insurance, after the war, I had to type out all my own policies. Couldn't afford a secretary. I didn't have the luxury of a computer." He held up a hand and wiggled his fingers. "These digits may not be as fast as they once were, but they still work. It's important I still do things on my own. Please understand. I do appreciate your offer to help."

"Okay," Katie acknowledged. "I just can't imagine anyone wanting to use a typewriter." She turned back to her computer and opened a file on her desk.

Satisfied that his niece was lost in her work, Jake pivoted his chair around. "I think one label should be plenty."

"No," Eunice disagreed. "Most people wouldn't bother for one. It has to be at least three."

"Give me some room then." He laced his fingers together, then pushed them out in a stretch in front of him as if warming up to play the piano. "I'll need silence, too."

The four of them watched as Jake painstakingly typed each letter. He consulted the paper with Loretta's address, then pecked out a letter or a number. It took extraordinary self-control for Eunice *not* to say anything. Inside, she was screaming for Jake to get up and let her type. She might not be an expert, but she was faster than him. The trembling started at her fingers and worked its way up to her shoulders, then shot down her torso to her feet, which begin to tap. Jake stopped typing, and Gus leaped into action, pulling a protesting Eunice from the room.

"Why did you go and do that?" Eunice pushed Gus's hand away, causing some curious looks from strolling residents.

"I had to. You were about five seconds away from blowing your top and having your say. You should know by now that Jake isn't exactly as tolerant as yours truly."

He had a point. However, Eunice didn't want to admit it. Instead, she exhaled audibly and glared back at the gawkers who had slowed down to stare at them. This hurried most of them on their way, but not all.

One blue-haired resident stopped in front of Eunice with a genial expression and announced, "I can't wait for the barn dance. It's been decades since I've kicked my heels up. Might not be kicking so high, but I appreciate the opportunity. You're amazing." The woman gave Eunice a pat on the arm before resuming her walk.

Gus gave her a nudge. "Who's that?"

Truthfully, Eunice didn't know the woman. "Someone who thinks I am amazing."

"Barn dance?" Gus responded and raised his eyebrows.

Obviously, the man had heard most of the conversation. He'd been standing close and the brilliant woman who had the good sense to recognize Eunice as amazing hadn't exactly whispered her comments, either.

Now there had to be a barn dance or people would be disappointed. Worse, she'd look foolish. It might do her good not to be out in public view where more people would inquire about the promised dance. "I think I better check on Kitty."

"You haven't decided on a solid name for the cat yet?"

Good question. Her shoulders went up in a shrug. "How about Oreo?"

"It makes him sound like a cookie. Someone might try to take a bite out of him." Gus chuckled at his own clever wit.

It wasn't funny at all, but it did make Eunice shelf the name. "I guess I'll go with Domino. Come and get me when Jake actually finishes." Excited about seeing Domino, Eunice almost skipped to her room, but she forced herself to maintain a sedate pace as to not attract attention. When she reached her room, the door was ajar. Oh, my stars! Her heart skipped a beat as she pressed a hand to her chest. What happened? "Who's been in my room?"

A woman dressed in a blue custodian uniform pushing a house-keeping cart out gave a derisive snort. "You should thank me. Your room stinks to high heaven. Now, I know you want to take care of your room on your own, but some priorities have to be observed if we don't want the health department closing us down. I emptied your trash, but you need to throw out whatever you got hidden in that room that smells so bad. I wasn't going to look because they don't pay me enough for *that*." The woman finished her statement by placing a fisted hand on her well-rounded hip.

Tamping down her urge to tell the woman she had no right to be in her room, she mumbled, "Okay." Next time, she'd make sure to lock her door. The keys were mainly for the residents' sense of well-being since the nursing staff had master keys for whenever someone locked themselves out or lost their key.

The custodian moved down the hall, as quick as the speed of a sloth, as Eunice kept her eye on the cracked door. Once the woman went around the corner, Eunice made a thorough survey of the hallway for Domino before darting into the room. She closed the door and leaned against it. Talk about a day and it wasn't even close to being over. After a couple of well-earned deep breaths, she shifted into action. "Domino, Mommy's home. It's safe to come out now."

No results. Of course, the cat didn't know his name yet. "Here, kitty, kitty."

Nothing again. What if he escaped the room? Worse yet, what if he went out one of the doors that were constantly opening and closing with the endless stream of employees, vendors, and the occasional visitor? An uneasy sensation started in her stomach and worked its way up to her throat. It felt like she couldn't breathe.

A single knock sounded before Gus stuck his head in the door. "We're ready to go. Jake's done." He took one look at Eunice's horrified expression and slid into the room. "What's wrong, sweetheart? You almost look as if you've seen a ghost."

A ghost would have been preferable. She opened her mouth to speak, but could only say a couple of words. "Cat. Gone."

Instead of looking as anguished as she felt, Gus raised his eyebrows. "You tried calling him?"

"I did." Surely that would convince her sweetie of the horror of the situation. While she knew she wasn't great at making friends, she had hoped to do better with a cat.

"Don't fret. Cats aren't dogs. They don't come when they are called. Could be he doesn't know his name, either, since you've called him about a half a dozen so far. Got any tuna left?"

Her heart slowed a little as she pondered Gus's words. What if the man was right? She hoped he was right. "I do," she squeaked and pushed off from the wall to retrieve the requested item. After opening a can of tuna, she handed it to Gus, who placed it on the floor near the bed skirt. He held a finger up to his lips. They waited in silence until a black and white feline head poked out from under the bed to see what offering the human servants had brought him.

It was going to be all right. She hugged Gus, mentally promising not to disparage the man in public or in her mind. "You're my hero."

"Heh, heh." He chuckled. "I like the sound of that." They stood embracing for a few seconds as the cat noisily chomped down on his fishy entrée. Finally, Gus spoke, "You need to bring some junk mail. We need to find three probable pieces of mail we can put the stickers on. Stuff like Dear Occupant and such. I doubt the husband will read them, but just in case."

"You're so smart." She cooed the words, sounding like a love-struck school girl.

"Ah," Gus hesitated and colored up some. "Lola thought of the mail idea, not me."

"No, I don't mean the mail. I mean finding my cat." She gave him a peck on the cheek that deepened his flush.

"I bet you can do anything. Even help me with a barn dance that now has to happen." Her faith was suddenly absolute in her man.

"I'm almost afraid to ask. What do you need me to do to help?"

Eunice laid her head on his shoulder and walked her fingers up his arm the way she remembered movie sirens doing. "Nothing much, really. We need a barn. A clean one without the animals where we could hold a dance. We need transportation to the barn as well as convincing administration to allow us to have the dance to begin with."

"That's all? Huh?" He took a deep breath. "We'll get it done—somehow."

Chapter Fourteen

G US AND EUNICE caught up with the other sleuths in D wing. The other three were off to the side clutching various pieces of junk mail and talking. A white envelope bent as Jake waved it. "This won't do at all. It's for some charity in Vegas."

Lola rolled her eyes at the man's theatrics. "What do you expect? I'm from Vegas. Besides, charities can be anywhere."

"I understand that," Jake concurred, but brandished the envelope for all to see. "I think Robert would have a hard time believing his wife contributed to or was interested in giving to the retired gamblers' rest home."

"Who knows? Loretta could be a gambler. Most people assume gamblers rake in a ton of money. Most don't. They make a little here and there. Usually, they go through it just as fast trying to fool women that they are more successful than they really are. Where's *your* mail?"

Jake handed the envelope in question back to Lola and mumbled, "I don't have any."

The former showgirl gave a small sniff, but Gus, who may not have heard the reply, asked, "What did you say?"

Knowing he'd have to repeat it again if he wasn't clear the second time, Jake slowly enunciated the words, "I have no junk mail. I throw away my junk mail as any thinking person would do."

A series of sniffs, snorts, and one gasp indicated not only had the barb found its mark but also that everyone else had indeed brought mail. Eunice felt the attack was unwarranted as she withdrew the envelope she had in her pocket. "I did my homework and brought mail. It's one of those numerous ads for furniture. They write you a letter to let you know that out of the thousands of people in the area, you happen to be the lucky occupant to get a ten percent discount, which isn't much when you consider furniture is marked up five hundred percent from the wholesale price. I think it's feasible she'd get an ad like that."

The rest of them agreed, and one of the address label stickers went on the envelope. Eunice made sure the rectangle covered up any of the former address. She also noticed the name was spelled wrong. "You spelled Simmons with one M."

"Makes it look more authentic." Jake gave a sage nod. "All these folks that are selling folks' addresses are bound to make mistakes."

"Sure, but it had nothing to do with your typing?" Eunice was miffed she hadn't typed the labels. It certainly would have taken her half the time it took Jake, even with her arthritis. Gus felt like it was a way they could include Jake. Although no one ever bragged about the man's typing skills, including the man, he bragged about plenty.

Instead of taking insult, he merely lifted his chin higher, the better to give an imperious stare down. "We are going to be handing the husband three letters that were supposedly misdirected to our house. Wouldn't it be odd if all the label stickers looked exactly alike? It would be almost as if someone slapped them on there."

The man had a point. It was a good one, too. Maybe he really had been a spy. Still, she wasn't discounting bad typing. Jake could be equally skilled in creating excuses. They rejected envelopes for male-oriented products such as mustache wax and campaign mailers from various candidates. No one would bother trotting over election mailers since everyone got those. Finally, they decided on an offer to refinance their mortgage that Herman furnished and a blue envelope from a real estate organization Lola provided.

Ever curious, Eunice held the blue envelope up to the light. "Selling your house?"

"Ha." Lola wrinkled her nose, well aware of Eunice's prying tendencies. "We all had to sell our homes to get in here. No. I worked in real estate after my showgirl career. The end result is I'm always getting mailings from various real estate groups. Sometimes, it's to announce some training opportunity. Other times, it's a listing of nearby homes."

"Your name isn't on it, is it?" Eunice queried. They had talked about the need to keep the mail impersonal just in case Robert decided to read it. He might read them to see if it gave a clue where his wife might have gone or was incriminating, depending on his possible guilt."

"Not my name. It's addressed to the current homeowner. I imagine the letter inside starts out *Dear Homeowner*. It will serve. Even if it was mailed from Nevada, who knows what mail Loretta might have been getting when she and Robert lived together? If the man decides to take a sudden trip, that would be telling."

Telling *what* would be the more important question. Would he be heading out west to find his wife or locate anyone whom Loretta may have told too much information? It was time for them to head out. Previous exits had taught them that going out in a group sparked too much attention. Instead, they usually slipped out of the home in dribs and drabs and met at Herman's car.

"Okay," Herman announced, holding out his crooked arm for Lola. "I'm taking my girl for a walk."

In code, that meant he and Lola would simply be stepping outside without any sneaking around just for the simple opportunity to get a breath of fresh air and privacy. Jake gave a short salute and slipped away. No one knew how Jake exited. Perhaps he ducked into a custodian office or unoccupied room and climbed out the window.

Eunice cut her eyes to her sweetie. "That means we get the courtyard."

"Again?" Gus gave a small groan as he gestured to the double glass doors leading to the courtyard. Before Eunice could take a step, the activity director called out. "Wait up!" The woman bustled up with a huge grin. "I hear we're having a barn dance. I'd love to hear about it. I have to run the details past administration. Protocol, you know."

"Aw…" Eunice stalled. She had nothing. On any given day, she would have a multitude of excuses and alibis. "Well, ah, I…"

Gus waved both hands as if trying to distract a charging bull. "We can't even talk about a dance until we get some of the residents dancing. No dancers mean no dance."

"I see your point," the activity director agreed, but then, cocked her head and added. "I think the *promise* of a dance would encourage more dancers."

It had been Eunice's initial thought, so she had to respect the woman's logic. "I'm working on it. It can't be too far in the future. I'll let you know as soon as I have details." She hoped it would be enough for the busy director and she'd move along. By now, everyone else was on their way to the car or already there.

"Do that. I need to get set up for movie heart-throb bingo." She gave a wave and took off at a good pace down the hall.

Gus echoed her words with a puzzled mien. "Movie heart-throb bingo?"

"Don't ask." She grabbed her sweetie's arm and towed him to the courtyard doors. Most people assumed the courtyard was self-contained with no exits. After spending so much time in the place having sleuth meetings and practicing shuffleboard, they discovered a gate that was hidden by an aggressive rambling rose. It was no easy feat to get by with the bush catching clothes and skins with its barbed thorns. Only the small in stature could manage it, which was why it was Eunice and Gus who had to use the gate.

Once in the car, they discussed plans not to park on the street, which might cause someone to recognize the dated sedan. That was Herman's worry. Personally, she thought two unknown geezers hiking around the neighborhood would be more noticeable. Since she lost the vote, she and Jake hiked to Robert's house.

Her companion was always one to point out the obvious. "There's no guarantee the man will be there."

"Yep." She had thought of that. Lance had said something about his being an accountant. Tons of people were working from home nowadays since it saves money on not having an office. With any luck, Robert might be one of those. They also didn't know his schedule. One thing she had learned since taking up with the sleuths was that most fact-finding missions were dead ends. What they usually found out was where *not* to look.

A small compact car was in the driveway of their target house.

She gave Jake a nudge. "Hey, look at that."

"Doesn't necessarily mean anything. He could have two cars."

"Loretta took one."

He gave an audible exhale. "I know. That car might not be running, and he had to get a ride to work."

"Please. Talk about taking the negative side. What's wrong with you? This is a stroke of luck." Eunice picked up her pace. Robert might be there now, but it didn't mean he'd be there forever. He could be late for work or had come back to pick something up. She wasn't totally sold on the working from home theory. As senior sleuths, their hours were limited when they could solve crimes. There were no midnight stakeouts or pre-dawn raids. No, they'd leave that to the boys in blue. "Hurry up!"

Jake's long legs allowed him to lengthen his stride with ease, although he grumbled as he did so. "Why are you so excited about confronting a killer? He could kill us both."

Even though Gus had included his old war buddy in their current sleuthing, the man still held to his belief that Loretta was dead. *Geesh*. Some people could be insanely bullheaded. Luckily, she wasn't like that. "I know that's what you think. Even if it was true and he did kill his wife, it would be because he had a personal reason. We are two innocent strangers. He has no reason to kill us. Besides, if he did it in this neighborhood, there would be witnesses. The man must know the police are watching him."

The house and car loomed closer. Red and yellow plastic flowers sprouted from the decorative planters on the porch. Loretta's touch, Eunice deduced. A man who hated his wife would destroy any evidence of her handiwork. Still, a clever killer would leave the plastic plants as a sign of his supposed grief. Now she was taking Jake's view. Lance talked about the man being quiet and inoffensive—usually what every neighbor said about the serial killer who lived next door.

On one crime drama, Eunice remembered the wife commenting on finding out that her husband had murdered twenty-two young women when he had been the best husband she ever had. It made Eunice wonder about the other husbands. Maybe they hadn't worked at putting on a front. Would Robert play at being someone he wasn't? Better yet, had he done it for years? Loretta's letter complained about how bland their lives were. Boring wasn't a crime. If it were, most of the general population would be locked up. Not her, of course. No one accused her of being boring.

Outspoken, yes. Nosy, yes. Mettlesome, a definite yes, but never boring. "Here we are," she needlessly announced the obvious. "Get your letters ready."

The open curtains and a glass security door allowed them to see inside the house. White walls, a brown plaid living room suite that had seen better days and a wood coffee table. A couple of uninspired landscapes decorated the wall—the kind you'd find in every room of a cheap motel. It wasn't exactly a magazine layout. Both she and Jake stood on the porch that boasted two folding chairs.

Jake may have been reluctant to knock while Eunice mentally catalogued the living room furnishings. Not quality items by a long shot. More likely, it was warehouse furniture you picked up at a discount if you furnished your own truck to haul it away. There was a good chance a third of the homes in the neighborhood had similar furnishings. Still, something wasn't quite right about the room.

A balding man in short sleeves and khakis moved from a

backroom to the hall. He must have seen them because he backed up. Eunice hissed through clenched teeth. "Knock!"

Jake made a smart tattoo of a couple of knocks. The man inside hurried toward the door. It was hard to gauge his eyes since light reflected on his glasses, but his lips pulled into a ready smile. *Drats.* Lance had described him as an easy-going guy. According to neighbors, he didn't raise his voice despite any provocation from Loretta. Years ago, they would have called such a man *milquetoast.* Today, with an emphasis on hyper-masculinity, he'd be a wimp.

He opened the door. "So sorry. I didn't see you there at first. I had the radio on in the kitchen, which must have been the reason I didn't hear you."

Eunice returned his genial expression while the cogs turned in her head. The faint sound of a song playing in the background confirmed his story. His open face was empty of any suspicions, but he may be a very good actor. They had agreed that Jake would speak first since it would be more normal for a couple their age.

"No problem," Jake replied. "I think we've been getting your mail." He gestured behind him. "We live a couple of streets over. The street number is the same, which has probably resulted in us getting your mail." He held up the envelopes and read as if unfamiliar with the name, "Loretta Simons?"

"Simmons," he automatically corrected. "I'm Robert Simmons. My wife is Loretta." He held out his hand for the letters. "That's very kind of you to bring them over."

Interesting. Eunice kept her eyes trained on Robert's face, keeping what she hoped was a pleasant expression. The man didn't say his late wife or make any mention of her leaving. He could assume she was coming back. A man like himself might be willing to tolerate a great deal to be married to such a colorful female. Then again, if they didn't live directly on the street, there was no reason they would know his wife was missing. It could be Robert didn't want to broadcast the information.

Even though Robert had his hand outstretched, Jake parceled out the letters one at a time and commented on each one. "Looks like one of those mortgage offers." He slapped Herman's offering into the man's hand. "My wife and I got a reverse mortgage. The young kids might not like it, but it works for us."

Robert's gaze drifted down to the offering, then up to Jake. "I heard some good things about reverse mortgages."

There were some bad things, too, but the man made no mention of them, which meant he was kind or uninformed, possibly both.

Next was the furniture advert, which was passed to Robert, but not without comment. "My wife is always nagging me about new furniture. I bet your wife will see this and will want to rush out and buy all new stuff."

This caused Robert's smile to slip a little, and he glanced back at the sturdy plaid suit. "No reason to get new furniture. I bought this furniture twenty years ago, and it's still holding up."

Maybe she had been out of the furniture business for a while, but she was willing to bet the set was older than twenty years. Loretta was probably not a fan. It also told her the man pinched a penny until it screamed. Suddenly, it clicked. She knew what was wrong with the living room. There were no personal touches. No photos of vacations or family, no knick-knacks, and no souvenirs of special occasions sitting on any surface. It could be the man cleaned the place of Loretta's treasures and replaced them with nothing. There was one thing she knew: Loretta did not pick the couch. No thinking woman would have done that.

Jake held up the final envelope, "Looks to me like a real estate agent might be calling on you soon."

"I doubt it," Robert replied, taking the last letter. "Loretta keeps her real estate license active. So, we have no need for an agent. Thanks for your help." He gave a little wave, then closed the glass porch door, then the main wooden door, too.

"Looks like we have been dismissed. No good deed goes unpunished," Eunice commented to Jake, certain that they were being watched. "Let's head home. My soaps will be on before we get there if we don't hurry."

Chapter Fifteen

THE SLEUTHS CROWDED into the sedan talking all at once. Eunice was pleased with the results of the mail hand-off and couldn't wait to give the others the details—if she could get a word in edgewise. Jake was busy giving directions to a new eatery while Lola confided she bumped into the neighbor who had given her so much information before. It probably wasn't as good as hers.

Unfortunately, she heard herself asking, "What did she say? Did you trade tips on creating a Cleopatra's eye?"

"No," Lola answered as she buckled her seatbelt. "She did ask me if I had any of the three-wick candles with me. I had to apologize and tell her I merely made a delivery, but I would look for one. Then we got talking about Loretta. Surprisingly, she heard about the letter. I imagine the police have been asking questions."

Now they were getting somewhere. The car engine purred to life, and Herman directed the sedan onto the road. "Did you ask her if the police questioned her?"

"Of course not. That would be too obvious. I just let her talk. As I mentioned before, she told me Loretta had been in the cosmetic industry. She had sold a few things to our newest informant. In doing so, Loretta gave the impression she wasn't happy with her current life."

"How so?" While Eunice had to know, she didn't like that Lola may have garnered better information.

Lola turned to make eye contact with Eunice and shrugged her shoulders. "It wasn't so much words, but an *impression* that Loretta wasn't happy."

Really? That was it? "The yelling would have been a clue, along with the leaving."

"Exactly," Lola agreed. "If she was unhappy, then *she* would have done something about it, not her husband."

There was some merit to her logic. "Could be. Plenty of people have impulsively killed each other in an argument, especially when under the influence of alcohol or drugs."

A cough, and then a throat clearing suggested someone else had something to add. Jake coughed again, then said, "After meeting Robert, I had to withdraw my belief that Loretta is dead. That man wouldn't kill a mosquito."

Lola arched her penciled eyebrows. "You're a judge of killers?"

"Not normally," Jake answered in an amused tone. "Still, men have taken the measure of other men for years. Trying to decide if the other man might be a danger, an ally, or not important at all. It's how we have survived this long."

Such masculine posing made Eunice long to crack the window. Gus wanted him along, but she wondered if it was a wise move. He did do a good job interacting with Robert, though. She'd give him that. "You're saying the man is no danger to anyone?"

"Pretty much." Jake folded his arms, relaxed back into the seat and closed his eyes, indicating he had said all he needed to say.

The silence lasted for a few moments as Herman maneuvered his way through traffic. Neat houses with well-groomed yards gave way to small shops and the occasional church. Eunice recognized the landscape as leading to the business district. Obviously, they were heading to the restaurant first. Even though Eunice wasn't a fan of the dead Loretta theory, she was even less of a fan of Jake's smug certainty. He announced something, and it was like *that* was the end of things. No one second-guessed him, which she had to. It was her duty.

"Are you saying the man has no feelings? He never gets angry?"

Jake opened one eye, then the other. "Of course not. He gets angry, but he would never act on it. He might fantasize about it. He'd never do anything himself, though."

Listening to the man made him sound like a doctor on one of those crime shows, pontificating overlong on the nature of the criminal. Half the time, the doctors were wrong. Jake had no medical degree, either. His cockiness rubbed her the wrong way. "He could have hired a hitman."

Jake's eyes opened wider, and he sat up as straight as the seatbelt would allow. "That's a possibility I didn't consider." He slapped his head with the butt of his palm. "I can't believe I didn't think of that. Sometimes, the quiet ones will fool you."

That's what they always said on the true-crime shows, especially after they arrested the killer. In Eunice's opinion, they didn't fool the authorities too much, or they wouldn't have been arrested.

Lola turned to follow the backseat conversation, adding her two cents. "Hitmen are expensive. I wouldn't think Robert would have that type of money. Most hits are usually fifteen thousand, although some will drop it to ten thousand if it's strictly a shooting as opposed to making it look like an accident."

The way Lola so calmly delivered the pertinent information floored Eunice. Here she thought Lola's former life consisted of feathers, high heels, and conventioneers trying to cop a feel. Apparently, the woman had rubbed up against the dark side, too.

Gus had his eyes closed, making Eunice think he was asleep. It wasn't too unusual for the man to drop off into a catnap when sitting. It was never very long. As a courtesy, she never mentioned it. When he spoke, it surprised everyone.

"Lots of folks would work for a lot less. It doesn't mean they'll do a good job. In fact, if Loretta had been offed, I'd expect her killer to have been picked up by now. It makes me think she must still be alive and kicking."

Her sweetie had a valid point. A man who kept an ugly couch for more than two decades wasn't a man who would layout major money for a hit. He'd probably consider five hundred to be a great deal of money. As of yet, no one had asked her for the information she came up with. "Anyone want to know my impressions?"

There were several affirmative murmurs, but since they were coming with her soliciting them, it made the impressions practically worthless. All the same, she'd give the sleuths the benefit of her observations. "Here's what happened." She borrowed the line from a popular television detective. "Robert is cheap, which is reflected by his use of an old living room set that should have been burned years ago. He has an equally ancient table and not the valuable antique type, either. I noticed there were colorful fake tulips in the flower-pots that are more appropriate for the spring. It makes me think Loretta put them there.

"When I looked through the front window, I noticed there was nothing personal in the house. Just cheap prints. The same kind you find in roadside motels. I thought that was odd. There was no sign a woman had *ever* lived there. No knick-knacks. No photos. Nothing."

Instead of acting impressed at her deductive skills, Jake leaned forward to tap Herman on the shoulder. "The Happy Pelican is on your right."

Gus, who was becoming better at gauging her moods, patted her hand. "I'm sure the man got rid of her stuff."

"It's possible, but there were no sun-faded shadows where things *used* to be. Robert freely admitted he's had the couch forever. He kept the tulips. If he hated her so much, he would have ditched the flowers. If anything, it felt like there was no place for Loretta there. It wasn't a welcoming place. No wonder she left."

Chapter Sixteen

A FTER A DELICIOUS lunch of fried fish, fries, and cheesecake on a stick, which was pretty much all the things the Senior Sleuths' doctors had warned against consuming, they headed to the car for the shopping portion of the trip. A chilly wind forced them to pick up their pace as much as possible. Eunice reached the vehicle first, dragging Gus with her to no avail since it was locked. A backward glance confirmed that Herman was being a gentleman, keeping a leisurely pace with Lola and her walker.

Figures. A sigh pushed past her lips. When had she considered others before herself? Unlike the various blogs stating what it was like to live with a narcissist, Eunice didn't feel the bulleted items fitted her. Some might say she looked out for herself. In this world, she had to. Besides, she was used to being independent and didn't fancy asking folks to do for her. Most of the time, they didn't do for her, so she learned that lesson fast. Then there was her husband, the one she had to be grateful to for even proposing. Her nose wrinkled as she realized her first mistake was letting him know she was relieved he had asked.

Whenever she tried to express a different opinion on how something should be done, Dwayne, her husband, trotted out the fact that he had married her. He made it sound as if he was some Greek god who had lowered himself to aligning with a mere human. Somehow, the man had a greater sense of worth than he was entitled to. In fairness, he was a decent provider, not great, or she wouldn't have taken the furniture job. Part of the reason she took the position, besides money, was to be someone other than Dwayne's wife or her daughter's mother. She wanted to be her own person.

Maybe she had started too late on that process. It could have explained her perception that everyone was picking on her or out to get her. A steady diet of being told she was wrong by her husband whenever she expressed an opinion wore her down. Still, somewhere deep down, was an ember of a younger, feistier female that refused to die.

Her furniture job fanned the tiny ember. Her goal wasn't to get out of the house and socialize while earning a few bucks. No, it was survival. She knew eventually there would be no Eunice if she stayed with Dwayne, but she needed an income. With that in mind, she made herself into an indispensable employee and in the process, stepped on a few folks. She wasn't in the game to make friends. A funny thing happened while she worked on her secret goal of escaping. Dwayne died of a heart attack. The man was a fast-food junkie and always snacked after she'd made him a healthy dinner. What amazed her, besides being a sudden widow, was all the folks who showed up at the funeral and genuinely seemed to like Dwayne. At one point, she asked an attendee if he had wandered into the wrong viewing parlor. It seemed that way to her because they conversed about a man, she'd never met but shared a name with: her husband.

Eunice watched Jake, Herman, and Lola chatter as they strolled toward the car. They valued friendship more than their own comfort. Once Dwayne died, she threw herself into doing things her way since she had been denied the right for almost two decades. Sure, it was reactionary and a relief.

Fortunately, Herman arrived, unlocked the car, and cut short Eunice's reflections, for which she was grateful. In the car, they rated their meal favorably, then moved onto sleuth business. Lola pointed to Eunice with a lacquered nail as the car roared to life. "You really got me believing that Loretta is alive somewhere."

"I hear ya," Jake added, as he wiggled into the sedan's plush upholstery. He nodded his head in Eunice's direction "I agree with Lola. Sure, I wanted to think Loretta was dead. It seemed like the most obvious answer until Eunice pointed out those inconsistencies about the house. Then I got to thinking. Loretta's husband is a classic geek. He even had a plastic pocket protector."

The man wasn't saying anything Eunice didn't know. "Hey, I was there. I have to say the man checked all the boxes. He even had on his dark-rimmed glasses. The corner of one rim may have been repaired with black electrical tape, too."

"Good eyes," Jake complimented her, then tapped his nose. "Something doesn't smell right about this."

"Uh, that was me." Gus, who was squeezed between Jake and Eunice, said, "Fish makes me a little gassy. The baked beans I picked as a side probably didn't help, either."

Everyone, except Gus, groaned and Eunice cracked the window and waved her hand to dissipate a very real odor. Fish really didn't agree with her sweetie. However, Jake had to have meant something else. "What do you mean?"

Gus opened his mouth. "I thought you knew about my little problem when it comes to seafood."

"Not you. I meant what Jake was talking about." Her eyes rolled upward on their own. She blinked once, then again, trying to quell the old habit. A respected marriage counselor on an afternoon talk show stated eye-rolling was disrespectful and indicated the end of a relationship. "Sorry, sweetie, but I am curious what Jake meant."

Gus patted her hand. "No worries." He nudged Jake with his elbow. "Spill. Fill us with your wisdom."

"Not exactly wisdom," Jake responded with a shrug. "Just a simple observation. Even young boys are always trying to be cool. Whatever that means now. No one tries to act like a geek. Robert seems to thrive on doing so."

A chuckle came from the driver's seat. "I remember wearing those white buck shoes. They were made famous by a singing star. Everyone had to have them. My parents weren't into paying good money for shoes that kids intentionally scuffed up for the right look. There are probably worse things. Just look at all the kids with their ripped jeans and multi-colored hair. What's wrong with a guy who's okay with who he is?"

Nothing. It was something most people strived to be but never achieved. If that was Robert's situation, he was a lucky individual. Eunice played the brief interlude over in her mind. Nothing the man said or did was forced or awkward, but it did feel a tad inauthentic.

"You know," Lola added in an amused tone. "Being nerdish is kind of hot nowadays. Maybe our guy is in on the trend. Hipster or something."

"Hipster," Eunice repeated the word, liking the sound of it and the idea of Robert not reaching perfect contentment within himself. "Yeah, that's it. Robert gave us a few clues that may or may not turn out to be helpful. Your real estate letter prompted him to mention his wife used to be in the business. That could be a legitimate lead."

Lola snorted. "There's probably a thousand or more agents in the surrounding counties and another thousand in training. It's not exactly like we'll find the woman without a miracle, and that's only if she *is* in real estate. That online search also mentioned truck driver training and a nail technician license."

"Her husband didn't mention either," Eunice pointed out, rather proud of her observational skills. It was no wonder she could solve crime dramas before the fictional detectives did. It was all about the details.

The sedan slowed and pulled into the crowded parking lot of a well-known convenience store, which meant the conversation would be tabled. She would easily be able to break off from the group to furtively purchase her needed pet supplies.

Lola lifted one eyebrow as she turned in her seat to address Eunice. "Did you tell everything about your past to your husband?"

Actually, she hadn't, though not because she was secretive. There wasn't that much to tell, and Dwayne didn't want to know. Still, Eunice felt compelled to answer. "No. That means our only choice is to talk to the ex-husband, Jonas Hogg, if possible. We get information from Robert and the ex, then compare. Her ex might say something that Robert didn't. Now we'll have to decide on our cover. I'll leave that to you since you're so creative."

"Thank you," Lola responded. She blinked twice, possibly considering if the compliment had been genuine.

With a new pet, square dance lessons, and finding a barn for the hoedown, Eunice could use someone else thinking up covers. Who better than *Mary* who created her own showgirl façade and a new name to go with it? The woman acted genuinely pleased by the simple compliment. Life would have been much easier if she had known how well flattery worked.

Chapter Seventeen

A CLOUD PASSED over the sun, blotting out the somewhat wavery fall sunlight. The sleuths were in high spirits as they teased Gus about trying on several colognes in the store. Both Jake and Lola cracked the windows and mimed choking on the competing scents. Herman laughed as he drove but didn't bother to say anything. Eunice sat ramrod straight in her seat as an ominous feeling penetrated the car along with the sudden dimness. No one else appeared to notice. Instead, they continued to tease one another. Something was wrong.

Twisting in her seat, she noticed several cars behind them. No surprise there. Herman's slow and steady tortoise-like pace usually had people whipping around him. The double line prevented that, being so close to the nursing home, along with the cop who usually waited in the church parking lot for someone to make the dubious choice to cut into the shoulder to get by.

There were a few cars in the front lot, possibly visitors or salary employees who didn't have to clock in and took advantage of the front entrance, which was so much closer to the offices. The number of people visiting changed their entry methods. It wouldn't do to have them all sauntering down the halls like the opening of a television show. Criminals look out! The Senior Sleuths are in town. *Bold* was not their password. Instead, they usually tried to blend into groups exiting from activities or even the chaos of delivering meal trays.

"Low traffic," she announced the obvious and checked her watch. "Book Club is about to break up unless Ethel Farnsworth is in it."

A murmured agreement punctuated with a groan passed through the car since they all had tried the book club and had the experience of having the retired English teacher yammer on about metaphors and symbolism in whatever they read.

Jake yawned. "Just the thought of listening to her go on and on almost puts me to sleep. I wasn't a fan of school when I had to attend. It seems unfair that I have to get educated in my twilight years. I bet she can talk longer than it took the author to write the book."

"No one is making you go or listen," she reminded him. "Still, it makes our entry problematic if she's still going strong about the importance of certain colors or numbers in the latest selection. Herman and Lola can come in later or even go in the front door since there is no restriction on their movements. Jake, you could go in with them, but it might make you look like the third wheel. Gus and I are different matters altogether."

There was no need to add they were both on the equivalent of lockdown thanks to their concerned offspring. *Everyone* knew. Luckily, the staff had relaxed their vigilance since neither one of them made the mistake of being caught outside the building.

Herman eased in beside an oversized truck to hide his car and parked. Due to pushing the clocks back and eliminating an hour of afternoon sunlight, darkness fell faster, and the persistent cloud cover was no help. Even though it wasn't even three, shadows had popped up or deepened, which worked in their favor.

A slight wiggle of Eunice's thin shoulders did nothing to shake off the prickling sensation that climbed up her back. The best thing to do was to get inside. They could make plans to discuss their next move after she set up Domino's goodies. Her kitty would be so pleased. It was time to put their exit into action. Even though no one ever appointed her leader, she often took up the mantle on her own. On occasion, the other sleuths allowed her to keep it for little matters such as this.

"Okay, sleuths," she barked in an overloud voice. "Here's the plan. Jake can go first. His being alone shouldn't raise any eyebrows. It might be nice if you drop into the book club if it's still going."

"No." Jake pushed out the word and folded his arms, making his feelings known about that particular diversion.

She moved on, aware the man would not be convinced. "All right, Gus and I together might attract too much attention, with rumors flying the way they have been. I'll go in ahead and act angry while Gus trails behind."

Jake had the nerve to raise one eyebrow. "How is that different than your usual entrance?"

Great Scott! They'd be here all day if Jake was going to question everything she said. It did make her do a quick recounting. Was she usually angry? Was Gus in the dog house most of the time, not quite sure how he got there? She didn't have time to dwell on that. Besides, Jake was only trying to needle her. The more time they spent around one another, the better he became at knowing what buttons to push. *Ignore, ignore,* she mentally prompted herself.

"Of course, Herman and Lola can go in whenever they please as long as they're last. Let's go. This must be what it's like running those covert military missions," Eunice mused and rubbed her hands together.

Jake loosened his seatbelt, swung open the car door, and placed one foot on the pavement. He took time to glance back at Eunice and make eye contact as he spoke, "It's *nothing* like Special Ops missions."

Oh, she knew that. Just like she knew he'd respond to her comment, confirming what everyone wanted to know. It sounded to her like their Jake knew his way around a few covert missions. Good. His experience would be valuable in tracking down someone who didn't want to be found. The vehicle blocked her view of the side door, which meant she had to rely on her watch as it counted off three minutes. Once the minute hand made its third sweep, Eunice depressed the door handle. "Remember, wait at least a minute. Not too long since you're supposed to be behind me." Feeling like she should do it, she made a downward motion with her hand and gave herself the order, "Go!"

She scurried in a hunched posture as she skirted the cars, even surprising a kissing couple in a low-slung sports car. Eunice didn't slow down to see who it was but did notice the uniform colors. Blue for housekeeping and white for dietary—it shouldn't be too hard to turn up some names. That was if she had time. The important thing was for them not to see her. Of course, she'd be just another old lady to them, unrecognizable from the rest of the female residents.

Inside, she hurried to her room, ignoring Gus calling her name. He'd meet her in the room. While Gus was easy to evade, it wasn't as easy to duck the activity director, who had to have cloned herself because she was everywhere. "Eunice! I was looking for you."

Since breaking into a mad run wouldn't work with her plan to attract as little attention as possible, she stopped. "Oh, you were. Whatever for?"

"Emergency meeting of the square dance committee." The director consulted her watch. "It's at three-thirty, so, about twenty minutes. Pearl asked that you meet in her room since it's so close to dinner. You know how some of the residents can be."

Yep, she knew. Many started rolling into the dining room an hour or more before the meal was served. Even though seats couldn't be reserved, most knew that specific residents laid claim to certain tables. It would be theirs until the day they died. Pearl knew enough not to try to use the dining room as a meeting place so close to mealtime. The residents not only kept watch over their tables but socialized by yelling questions to one another. Add in the clatter of the pans from the kitchen and it was almost impossible to hear. As much as she hated to admit it, Pearl made a wise choice.

"Got it." She stuck out her thumb on her free hand as an acknowledgment that she'd be attending the meeting. She had to. Otherwise, Pearl would report her, but more importantly, the bossy woman would take over without someone to rein her in. Her lingering in the hallway allowed Gus enough time to catch up. He waved at the activities director as she strolled by, obviously in search of another resident to inform or manipulate into doing something she'd rather avoid.

Gus moved up beside her and asked in a loud whisper, "Are we still fighting?"

"I guess not." She blew out a long breath, fairly certain no one paid a lick of attention to her angry walk. Maybe she had done too many angry walks, or it could be people weren't that interested in what was happening with other folks since they were too focused on their own lives. It might be both. "I can use your help. We need to get Domino's thing set up before I go to the meeting. You can play with him while I'm gone."

"Got a laser pointer?" he asked with a wink.

"I don't, but I did buy a stick with a ribbon on it. You need to dangle that in front of the cat. They like that. Of course, you've got to move around to keep it interesting," she explained, certain the man knew nothing about cats. The store had so many great toys for felines, but she had to keep her expenditure reasonable to keep her daughter from questioning it and calling the center to ask about it. Thank goodness she took the precaution of setting up another bank account that no one but herself knew about. It was her emergency fund. A girl had to have some money to call her own. She hadn't even told Gus about it.

When they turned the corner, it appeared as if her door was open. That couldn't be right. It had to be the light. She had made a point of locking it, but any nurse or custodian could unlock it with a master key for the resident's safety or at least that is what they told the resident's family. Her fingers tightened around Gus's arm as she hissed, "Look."

"It's your room. The same place it's always been. What's the big deal?"

The door swung open and a custodian exited, carrying a toolbox and a plunger. He nodded in Gus and Eunice's direction. "Your room?"

"Mine," Eunice confirmed. She gestured in the direction of the room, not daring to ask the immediate question about the whereabouts of her cat. "What were you doing in my room?"

"Smell." He shrugged his shoulders. "I was told to check the plumbing. It's working fine."

Somebody save her from interfering busybodies. She closed her eyes and tried to count to ten, but only got to three before they popped open, and she darted for her door which was wide open and blocked only by the custodian. If Domino hadn't escaped already, he could easily run between the man's legs. "You just got started on my room?"

"Nope." He gave a snorted laugh, rather pig-like if pigs laughed. "I call it a continuing project. There was the short in the fire alarm on Wing E. Surely you heard them going off?"

Oh, my goodness. If they'd evacuated the place, they'd have found out the sleuths were missing. "Fire drill?"

The man shot her an odd look.

That's right. She would have been here and should have known about it. "I hate when those fire alarms malfunction, especially during bingo." They played so much bingo at the center there had to be a form of the game going on somewhere.

It was almost as if the man hadn't been interrupted and dropped right back into his narrative. "I wasted two hours on that, then it was lunchtime. Just got back to your room. No issues that I can see."

"Ah good." She had to look up to address the man. "Well, I need my room now. Good day."

"Yeah, good day to you, too," he offered, then lumbered down the hallway, possibly to his next project.

Gus scooted in before she shut the door. "Help me look." Eunice gasped the words, flung her shopping bag on the bed, dropped to her knees, and peered under the bed. "It's so dark under there. I can't see anything. We should move the bed."

The feeling of dread she had felt in the car returned. Who knew she and her newfound pet were psychically connected? She must have felt him leave or maybe it was the fear Domino felt when a stranger came into the room. She gripped the headboard and pulled herself into a standing position.

Gus positioned himself by the footboard on the other side of the bed and started to push. "Geesh, this bed is heavy. It isn't moving much." He managed to grunt out the words.

Eunice released her hold on the headboard and stepped away from the bed. Gus swung the end of the bed about four feet before stopping. "Wow! What did you do? It was so much easier that time."

No time to tell him he was pushing against her. Instead, her eyes dropped to the exposed items, which included her makeshift litter box, a sweater she put down for Domino to use, and a mystery novel she had started, but promptly lost. Eunice bent over and picked up the book. "No cat."

Her shoulders drooped. It was a far-fetched plan that she would be able to have her own personal kitty. It would have been nice if it lasted a little longer. She never even got to sit in the rocking chair with the kitty on her lap. "It's over. He's gone."

"No, wait." Gus rooted through the bag on the bed and withdrew a small tin of cat food. "Let's open this and leave it on the floor. It's bound to lure him out of his hiding place."

It was a nice gesture, but she knew her cat was gone. The room felt different, less warm, less homey. What she'd like to do was have a good cry. Kind of hard to do with Gus in the room because he'd try to fix her as if she was a doll missing an arm. She almost never allowed herself the luxury of sobbing. Now wasn't the time, either. She consulted her watch. It was time to rein in Pearl before the woman took control of the committee.

"Gus." She whispered his name, too drained to do much more. "I gotta go. Meeting. I would appreciate it if you would stay and wait. Just in case." Eunice didn't dare clarify what she meant, afraid that speaking the words might cause it not to happen, rather like not announcing your birthday wish before you blew out the candles.

Her sweetie covered the space between them and wrapped her in a tight hug.

Eunice stood limp in his embrace, but still appreciative. "Thank you. I'll be back as soon as I can."

As she left the room, she pulled the door closed, just in case. Sometimes, miracles do happen. She read it was all about setting intentions. That's what she would do. Her fists tightened as she took a deep breath and wished hard for her beloved feline to be safe, warm, and well cared for. After all, it wasn't what she needed. It was more about what her four-legged friend needed.

Feeling somewhat calmer, she strolled purposefully toward Pearl's room. She didn't need to ask where it was since she had strolled the length of the facility hundreds of times and knew where every nook and cranny was. Pearl's door was decorated with a huge wreath adorned with silk flowers and a menagerie of birds that never would have co-existed in real life.

With each step, she rehearsed what she might say if asked about her plans to get the barn. There was the classic one—she-was-working-on-it. Then the bald-faced lie, which was saying it was in-the-bag accompanied by polishing her nails on her shirt. If all else failed, she could do the there-have-been-issues one. That allowed her to pull the plug on everything or be a hero when things did work out since people were expecting otherwise.

Carmen met her where the hallways intersected. The woman grinned at Eunice. "I bet we're going the same way. Let's hurry. Pearl told me she had a big surprise. I can't wait. It could be cupcakes."

"Sure, let's go," Eunice replied without the tiniest bit of enthusiasm. This is what their lives had devolved to. A promise of a cupcake brightened the day. However, Eunice did like cupcakes, especially the filled ones, and her pace picked up.

Carmen gave a slight knock and pushed the door open. Pearl was sitting contently in her bentwood rocker gently rocking back and forth petting a black and white cat. *Domino.* She was petting Eunice's cat.

"You need to move so I can close the door," Carmen informed Eunice.

She took a side step to allow the door to close, but that was all she *could* do as mentally she lambasted the universe. Sure, she wanted her cat safe, warm, and happy, but she did not want her in Pearl's lap. Next time, she'd have to be clearer in her intentions. Dagnabit, she'd have to steal her cat back.

Chapter Eighteen

E UNICE STARED AT Pearl's hand as she stroked the cat. The creak of the rocker was almost deafening. On one hand, Eunice knew it wasn't that loud, but everything about the situation was overwhelming, including the heat. What did she have the heat set to? Charbroiled? She could hear the women talking. Carmen spoke in a light, fluttery tone, but Pearl's voice was more like a sledgehammer, pounding things into the ground or more likely, crushing dreams with each word.

She heard her name, which meant they addressed her. There had to be some way she could get her cat back. A half-dozen scenarios popped into her mind and left just as quick, especially considering she didn't have a time machine or a space ship to send Pearl on a trip to the great beyond. Instead, she'd have to rely on the wits that had gotten her this far. Never mind whatever they asked her, she decided to go for the real issue. "Can I hold your cat?"

Pearl gave the slightest of nods and before she could complete it, Eunice had swept the cat off her lap and draped him over her own shoulder. Her hand went over the smooth fur in comforting strokes as she slowly walked the room. "What's his name?"

"Chairman Meow."

Ugh. Something cute and punny. The very idea had Eunice mentally apologizing to the cat for the indignity. Well aware she had to play the possibly best long game of her life, she replied, "Clever."

Pearl pumped up with pride. "I thought so, too." The woman rocked a few times with a pleased expression on her face before speaking. "Okay, girls. We got to get things in gear. I heard the Square Dance Team is willing to be here twice a week. I suspect it will only take us a month to get the residents do-si-do-ing and promenading." She pointed to Eunice. "You'll need to get Gus here, along with Herman and Jake. Due to the ratio of men to women here, it's obvious many of us will be dancing with other women. Still, it would be nice to occasionally have the experience, no matter how short-lived it might be, to dance with a man."

Did she hear the woman right? Eunice's job was to round up the men she knew well, including her own sweetie, and make them the equivalent of Hurley Burley girls who dance with miners for a nickel? Of course, the major difference would be the men wouldn't get paid a nickel or otherwise. Pearl said the words as if she believed Eunice would do it. The woman had more faith in Eunice's gifts of persuasion than she did. If, by chance, she got the men to actually show up, she could not promise to make them dance. Jake would because he loved being the center of a group of admiring females. Gus might if she asked him. If Herman decided to trip the light fantastic with another, it would only be at Lola's urging. Come to think of it, she really could do it.

Normally, she bristled at Pearl giving orders, but as long as she was waving her hands and pointing, Eunice could hold onto her beloved Domino. It was no wonder he decided to explore the center. Hiding underneath a bed with a makeshift litter box was no life for a pet. A visual survey revealed no litter box or cat bed, just two small bowls on the floor, one filled with water and the other empty. Eunice had the supplies for a cat while Pearl had none. There had to be a way to broker a deal. They each had what the other needed.

Pearl's voice broke into her musing. "How's the barn situation going?"

"Fine, fine," Eunice hurried to reassure. It was always best to act like something was already a done deal. She could have read that sentiment in a sales memo, but it tended to work. People usually bought into whatever a confident person was selling. "Of course, we'll have to settle on a date. I might talk to Bob and Debbi about the musicians. It's not as easy as you might think, finding a square dance caller. They aren't thick on the ground, you know."

They *might* be thick on the ground, but she didn't know and was willing to bet Pearl and Carmen didn't know, either. At least it sounded like she was working on it, and she was. Hadn't she mentioned it to Gus?

Carmen, who had mainly watched the back and forth dialogue between Pearl and Eunice, finally spoke up. "I have a cousin who's a caller. He even took a course and everything. I bet he would be glad to do it."

Just like that, an answer to her problem tumbled right into Eunice's lap. "Does he have a barn?"

"What?" Carmen did a double-take.

Maybe she shouldn't have said that. Eunice managed an apologetic smile. "Just joking. Your cousin doesn't have a barn."

"Oh," Carmen's eyes rolled upward as she tried to remember. "It's been a while since I've been out to Cousin Eddie's place. I think he has a barn, but it's probably crammed with stuff. Eddie's a bit of a hoarder."

"Don't worry about it," Eunice said. She waved her free hand as if sending the possibility of using Eddie's barn on its way. It didn't help that Pearl was giving her the fisheye. A distraction was called for. "Is administration okay with your having your own personal pet in your room?"

Instead of replying, Pearl looked away. She rocked a little harder without saying anything. Finally, she stopped her agitated rocking and fixed a baleful look on Eunice. "Are you going to tell? I wouldn't take you for a squealer."

This was the opening Eunice needed, and she had to make the best of it. She continued to stroke Domino. "I'm not a squealer. In fact, I wouldn't mind having a cat of my own. It makes me understand your wanting one. I know the center has its own cat, but it isn't the friendliest kitty. Could be because too many people have handled it. I'd not only be willing to help you, but I'd love to share cat owner responsibilities with you. I might even be able to round up some cat supplies."

Pearl gave Eunice a considering look, then started rocking again. As Eunice waited, Carmen sidled closer and explained. "It's her thinking chair. You can tell what type of mood she's in by how she rocks."

That didn't tell her too much. Eunice knew she needed to do something to sweeten the deal. Sharing the cat with Pearl wasn't exactly the dream she had in mind. The impulse to let the cat in hadn't been something she'd thought out. She saw the cat and wanted it. True, she knew the administration would take a dim view. That much she did know. What she didn't consider was how much time her sleuthing duties took.

People thought dogs needed people, but cats preferred the company, too. Maybe she and Pearl could share cat duties. It would demand a compromise from both of them. However, Pearl might think she was the one making all the concessions since she had control of the cat. It was time to remind Pearl what was at stake. Eunice walked to Pearl, waited for the rocker to stop, and placed the cat in her lap.

A tender expression crossed Pearl's face as she stroked the cat. "What would you get out of it?"

Progress. Not really success but possibilities. Still, she knew enough not to ask for anything yet. "It would make me happy imagining you petting Chairman Meow and rocking."

"Cut out the nonsense!" Pearl insisted with a lifted eyebrow. "I wasn't born yesterday. You want something so spit it out."

She expected a real song and dance routine but not this. It made Eunice respect the woman a little more. The best way to handle it would be as honest as possible. Not that she intended to confess to letting Domino inside. "I'd like visiting rights. I want to come by and pet our mutual cat. Maybe do so while using your rocking chair. I might want overnight visits, too."

Pearl stopped petting the cat and held her hand up. "Hold on. You're not staying overnight in my room. I don't care how much you love the cat." She shook her head. "Some people. You give them an inch and they go plumb crazy."

How could the woman get it so wrong! Eunice waved her hands in front of her making an X motion as if erasing the suggestion. She inhaled deeply, not wanting to say the name, but needing to. "No, I want Chairman Meow to stay at my place."

"Oh." Pearl cocked her head as if considering the suggestion.

"How would you get the cat to your room?"

"Trust me." Eunice placed her hand over her heart. "I can do it."

"Maybe." Pearl narrowed her eyes. "If you want the joys of pet ownership, then you have to shoulder some of the responsibilities."

Here it comes. Eunice expected as much. She'd play along until the right time presented itself and she'd liberate Domino. "What should I do?"

Pearl shrugged her shoulders. "Nothing much. It would be nice if you provided supplies and came by and cleaned the litter box. You have friends with a car. Maybe you can get our furry friend to the vet occasionally, too."

It sounded like Pearl expected her to do everything. She could agree, but that would raise red flags. "What exactly are you going to do? What's your contribution?"

Carmen, who'd been intently listening, added, "Yeah, what?"

Her outburst caused Pearl to glare at her friend before turning back to address Eunice. Apparently, the emotional turmoil was too much for the cat, who jumped from Pearl's lap to the floor and gave an annoyed swish of his tail.

"*I*," Pearl emphasized the word, "take all the responsibility of being caught with a cat in my room."

Really? That was it? Here Eunice almost respected Pearl, but the woman was even on par with her own clever machinations. "Nothing will happen to you. They won't kick you out. Only the cat would leave. It doesn't seem to me like you're risking much."

Eunice waited for objections. Instead, Pearl crossed her arms and her lips twitched up into a tight, superior smile. "My cat. My rules."

Chapter Nineteen

MUSIC POURED OUT of the dining room. Someone inside called out, "Everybody up! We're going to do the Virginia Reel to 'Polly Put the Kettle On.'" Herman hesitated at the entrance, "Why am I doing this again?"

Lola had managed to get the man there but with no guarantee she could get him inside the open doors. The best way to handle it was the element of surprise.

Eunice came up from behind and gave him a big shove. As she did so, she announced to the waiting female residents inside, "I've brought you a partner!"

Even though Herman might not be as popular as Jake, it didn't stop three women from grabbing his arm and squabbling about who he'd dance with first. He shot an anxious look at Lola, who smiled and said, "Have fun."

She nodded at Eunice. "And he will. Oh, he will claim it was misery, having the women fight over him. Why should Gus have all the fun?"

Inside, the group was working on basic steps. They had formed two lines and a person on each side of the line would skip to the center, grab the hand of another dancer, make a hundred- and eighty-degree turn, then drop hands and head into the opposite line. When it was Gus's turn, he skipped out to the center and swung his partner a little too hard. The woman managed to stagger to the other side without falling.

Even though it was amusing, Eunice pressed her lips together to not laugh.

A male voice asked from behind her. "What have I missed?"

She turned to stare up at Jake in all his glory. His hair was slicked back with pomade. Somehow the man had located a bolo tie and a pair of black cowboy boots. The cologne was a bit heavy, but she had a feeling that most of his partners wouldn't mind. "Not much. Except for Gus spinning his partner like a top. Go in there and show them how it's done."

"You bet." Jake sketched a salute before striding into the room. It was as if the air had changed, and it probably had, considering how much cologne Jake was sporting. The women immediately turned to see what was different. A few of the bolder women darted to Jake's side.

Lola nudged Eunice to get her attention. The amused blonde angled her head toward the dancers. "I'm going in to watch. With this walker, the best I can ever hope to do is slow dance while hanging onto a man's broad shoulders. It should be fun to watch. And you?"

Eunice popped up her index finger. "Give me a minute. There's something I need to do."

"All right. I'll save you a seat," Lola promised, then headed to the side of the room where all the tables and chairs had been relocated.

Another song came up about "My Gal Sal." Eunice found herself listening to the words and tapping her toe. She crossed her arms, leaned against the door mantle and watched Debbi, the teacher—resplendent in a pink square dance skirt and its many petticoats—

organize the dancers into groups of four. She then joined the other teacher, Bob, to demonstrate the steps.

Pearl, who had been watching the dancers, stood and headed toward the doorway. When she reached Eunice, she asked, "Why aren't you dancing?"

"Waiting on you."

"I'm here now."

Eunice refused to straighten up from her relaxed posture against the door. Instead, she tried to emulate Clint Eastwood in all those Westerns. Of course, she didn't have a gun, but she did have the attitude. "I see that. I dropped off the cat supplies."

"Appreciate it," Pearl acknowledged without showing a great deal of appreciation. It could be that was as happy as she ever got, which looked about the same as her normal slightly perturbed face.

"Men are here and dancing." Eunice felt obliged to point out the obvious.

"I noticed that, too." Pearl gave a small snort. "I had my doubts. I guess I shouldn't have considering the things you've done in the past. A couple of hesitant men are nothing to you."

It sounded like a compliment. She'd take it as such. "That's right. There isn't anything I can't do once I set my mind to it. When's visiting time with Chairman…" She winced, having to say the rest of the name. "…Meow?"

"Ah, a woman who gets right to the point," Pearl commented. She played with the cuffs of her sweater sleeves, adjusting one, then the other, pulling out the corner of a tissue, so it would be ready when needed.

She might appreciate a woman who got right to the point, but obviously, Pearl wasn't one. "So, when are my visiting hours?"

"Why not right after square dancing lessons?"

The thought of seeing Domino, whom she would make a point of calling by his rightful name to get him accustomed to it, was something she looked forward to. However, at the back of her mind was a slight inkling of something else she should be doing at that time. Oh yes, they were going to visit Loretta's ex-husband. They settled on posing as writers for a true-crime magazine. Lola wanted to be the interviewer and had insisted she looked the part. Even though the woman had given her an ample target to lob a zinger about the former showgirl being acquainted with the seamier aspects of life, she didn't. *Weird.* Eunice didn't like to think about it, but the woman was starting to grow on her.

"Truth be told, I have plans after square dancing. Why don't I keep him overnight?" The idea had popped into her mind, and it was a good plan. After all, how much could she cuddle and play with the cat with Pearl watching her from the corner like a discontented genie ready to turn her into a toad?

"Plans? Are you going to scrapbooking?" Pearl asked, showing a glimmer of interest. "Carmen likes that kind of thing, but it isn't my cup of tea."

"No to scrapbooking." *And another no to telling you what I'm up to.* Eunice turned to watch the dancers and hoped to end the interrogation.

"You going to get the barn dance nailed down?"

It wouldn't be beyond Pearl to try to tag along. "Gus promised me a surprise. I have no clue what it is. I *do*, however, have the barn situation under control. Do you think red gingham tablecloths will work?"

"We should have some blue ones, too. Not everyone is a fan of red. Too angry."

Eunice unfolded her arms to scratch her neck. It seemed like the thing to do. It kept her from talking. Right now, she was giving Pearl everything she wanted for cat visits, and the woman was taking advantage of it. So far, there had been zero visits. Pearl played the part of a difficult custodial parent to the hilt. When Eunice actually had the time to see Domino, Pearl had told her no. Since the cat didn't have an active social life, she didn't see what the problem was. Soon, it would be a moot point once she stole the cat back.

The only problem was she couldn't keep the cat in her room because Pearl would check. She wouldn't put it past her to question Gus, either. All she needed was a master key and information about Pearl's comings and goings. Carmen would be the go-to person for the last thing. It made her wonder how Pearl had managed to keep the staff out of her room. Right now, she had to lull the woman into a state of trust, which would be no easy feat.

"Blue sounds nice, too. Anything else you think would be good for the dance?" She hoped her voice sounded as genial as it did in her mind.

Pearl's eyes rolled up, and she sucked in her lips as she considered the matter. "Mason jars. We can put votive candles in them."

"The Fire Marshal wouldn't approve."

Instead of trying to fight the point, Pearl sighed audibly. "You're right. It'll have to be fake tealight candles. Not as bright, but they do create *some* atmosphere."

"I'll see what I can do," Eunice promised as she contemplated prices. Where did Pearl think the money was coming from?

"Good." Pearl gestured to the dancers. "I better get in there. I want to be ready for the dance. How about you?"

A memory flickered to life with Gus talking about how great a square dancer his wife was. It had breathed life into her competitive side. She should be dancing. Better yet, she had an idea, a wonderful plan. It all depended on Gus's family holding onto what was important, such as Gus's late wife Maureen's information on planning a hoedown.

Chapter Twenty

THE WIND WHIPPED the fallen leaves across the parking lot. In a few places, leaves lifted into a spiral. Eunice chafed her arms and stared up at the sky, noting the dark clouds gathering. It wasn't the best time to decide to drive somewhere they had never been. Crime never took a holiday, a day off, or confined itself to bright, sunny days. She'd known mostly what she was getting into when she wrangled her way into the Senior Sleuths. Mostly.

Some hound howled in the distance. It was a mournful wail. Appropriate for a scary movie, right after the main character is told not to go somewhere. Of course, the main character does exactly what he or she is told not to because otherwise there wouldn't be much of a movie.

Eunice watched Lola and Herman make their way toward the sedan. It felt as if they were in slow motion. When they met for a trip, they all took different routes so as not to attract attention. Perhaps, in the future, Lola and Herman should get a ten-minute— no, make it a fifteen-minute—head start. Jake stepped out from the shadow of a nearby SUV, startling Eunice, who jumped.

"Stop that! You just about took a year off my life."

"You don't have that many to spare either," Jake joked and got a slap on the arm in retaliation. "Come on, I was being sneaky. Isn't that the intent of us all slipping out from different places?"

"Yes." Eunice knew he had her, but she still didn't like being caught acting the fool. "It would be nice if you didn't scare us. If I'd screamed as opposed to jumping, someone would be bound to investigate."

"I didn't think about that," Jake admitted sheepishly and hung his head. "I'll do better next time."

"See that you do."

By that time, Herman and Lola had reached the car. Herman unlocked it and helped Lola into the passenger seat. After he stowed the walker in the trunk, he swung open the driver's door. "I'm so tired after square dancing, I'm not sure I have enough energy left to drive."

Not good. This would totally ruin their expedition. Eunice, who had already clambered into the back seat, leaned forward to announce, "I can drive."

Herman pushed out his chest as he spoke. "Suddenly, I'm filled with endless energy."

It sounded to Eunice like a slam on her driving. Gus must have thought so, too. "I still got my license. Why not let me have a go at the wheel? At least I'm familiar with the locale."

Herman climbed into the car, buckled his seatbelt, and started the car before answering, "Last time you drove anything you put a hole in the side of Donna's inn."

"It was a forklift. I'd never driven one before, which explains my inexperience."

A snort served as a reply, and Herman pulled his door shut. He glanced over to Lola, who had the address in her hand. She shook the paper and replied to the non-verbal question. "Jonas, the ex-husband, lives in Clarksville. We've been there before. Do you need directions?"

"Not until I hit Clarksville," Herman said, then turned on the headlights.

No one could ever say he wasn't a safe driver. More than one of them had grumbled about him going under the speed limit. All the same, Herman was the only one with a car, and they'd have to abide by his rules. Someone always had rules. Eunice couldn't remember a time she wasn't being told what she could and could not do. The worst part was she had no part in making the rules. It was no wonder she often wanted to break them or at least bend them.

"Does Loretta's ex know we're coming?" It was hard for Eunice to just go along when she wanted to lead the charge.

"Yes. It's an interview," Lola answered, rather matter-of-factly, as if she conducted interviews daily.

"Does he know *all* of us are coming? It's one thing to agree to an interview and you think it's one person, then have a troop of folks show up on your doorstep." A silence indicated maybe this whole scenario hadn't been thought through a hundred percent. Where was she when they were coming up with this plan? Probably at the painful committee meeting or trying to locate Domino. There needed to be a rule not to have discussions without all the sleuths present. Marci would enforce that rule, but since she had taken herself out of the loop and technically, they weren't really on a case, it was hard to do.

"Well…" Lola lengthened the word. "He may not know how many of us there are, but I didn't tell him it was just me."

"It would have been an assumption. A common one. That's what *I* would have thought." Once Eunice had found a hole in the plan, they'd made without her, she couldn't stop herself from pointing out the obvious.

Lola's brow was furrowed, and her mouth pursed as she turned to address Eunice. "Do you think it will be a problem?"

"Could be." She felt bad acknowledging what was apparent to her and to none of the others. "You'll be trotting five people into his house. He might not have enough chairs to seat everyone. His mind might start whirling, thinking things like why are all these folks in my house? Maybe, they're a gang of thugs."

"No," Jake interrupted. "He will not think we are elderly thugs. Do you know any elderly thugs?"

She didn't need Jake smoothing things over. "Not personally. It could be a thing. Jonas might think it's a thing."

Gus pointed to his forehead. "I could get Thug Life tattooed right there." He giggled as if he thought the possibility was hilarious.

Jake nudged his friend. "Not a good look."

"I was joking."

"I know." Jake held up one finger. "I want to go back to the interview. Eunice has a point. I doubt Jonas Hogg will fear for his life when he sees all of us. Younger folks sometimes have an irrational dislike of older people. They're afraid we might give their furniture that old person aroma of liniment and talcum powder. There's also the threat we might break out photos of the grandchildren and talk about them. It might be better just to have one person with Lola."

Eunice's hand shot up before she even realized it. "Me! Me! Me!"

"Why you?" Jake asked in a skeptical tone.

"Women are less threatening. We're more comforting and sympathetic." It almost looked as if Jake was buying it. She needed to think of other reasons. "Men don't want to trot out personal issues such as divorce in front of other men. It feels too much like the other men are judging them. Men always talk more openly around women."

"Hmm," Jake murmured as he stroked his chin. "She might have a point. Herman, what do you think?"

"I used to talk to my neighbor, Donna, a great deal. She was always offering me coffee and delicious treats." He made an *mmm* sound before continuing. "I sure do miss her white chocolate macadamia nut cookies."

Eunice was afraid Jake might not be able to read between the lines. "That's a yes."

"Let's ask the big guy," Jake said and nudged Gus. "What do you think of your woman going into the house with Lola?"

Gus winked at Eunice. "She'll protect Lola if anything goes south. She's fast and clever, not to mention the pepper spray she has in her purse. Make sure you keep your finger on the pepper spray, honey."

Eunice forced a laugh. "I had to get rid of it. The center can be weird about stuff like that. They consider it a weapon. Besides, I need my hands free to open doors for Lola and things like that."

Jake gave her a look that announced he knew she had pepper spray in her purse. So, what. Any smart woman would. "We can start a phone conversation in the car. Herman or Gus can call me. I answer, then put my phone in my pocket before we go in. That way you can hear everything that's going on inside, but it's important that you keep quiet. It works both ways. Jonas will be able to hear whatever you say. Even if he's okay with an interview, he might not be too happy with other people listening in."

A grumble came from the front seat. Lola leaned over the front seat to explain. "We're paying Jonas for the interview. He suggested it since something he might say could lead to the recovery of Loretta. Just like the tip lines you always see advertised on television."

Eunice had seen them, even tried calling a time or two, but her information never led to a conviction. Maybe it did and no one bothered to call her back or pay her. "You're paying him fifty dollars?"

"A hundred," Herman inserted the amount, sounding annoyed.

Herman always did seem to end up paying for a great deal. He had a right to be upset.

Gus cleared his throat. "You weren't around, so I paid your twenty."

Once they got to Clarksville, Lola turned on the phone GPS. A British accented woman's voice guided them into a humble neighborhood. The simple ranch homes had the look of neglect and loss of hope. Whoever owned them just gave up. Among the houses with crooked shutters barely hanging and torn screen windows stood one neat house. There were even plastic flowers in the flower box similar to the ones at Robert Simmons' home.

"This has to be it. Red and yellow tulips must be Loretta's trademark." Eunice pointed to the flowers while Lola consulted her phone. The car slowed as Herman maneuvered it next to the curb and parked.

"You're right. That's it," Lola agreed. She flipped down the visor and used the mirror to check her appearance. A quick touch up included blotting her nose with rice paper and reapplying her lipstick. "Oh no!"

"What?" Eunice suspected that Lola forgot her list of questions back at the center. "We can wing it. If you want, I can ask the questions. I have plenty."

"It's not that." Lola scrutinized her left hand. "The acrylic nail on my index finger is loose. If I don't get it fixed soon, it may rip off taking a part of my nail bed with it. After we get this done, we need to get it fixed right away."

Really? The woman was worried about her nail. Eunice regarded her own unpolished nails cut so short that no white showed. She understood Lola valued her appearance and had a weekly appointment to get both her hair and nails done at the center's salon. "Can't you take care of that when we get back?"

Lola sighed. "Have you tried to get an appointment at the salon?"

"No. Is it hard?" Whenever Eunice was convinced, she needed a haircut, which wasn't all that much since her hair didn't grow as fast as it once did, her daughter would swing by and take her to a hairstylist near the mall. As far as she could tell, they never even made an appointment.

"Impossible." She shook her head slowly. "There are more women who want services than employees to provide them. I'll never get in." A small moan punctuated her statement.

Herman turned to Lola and patted her hand. "It's okay, sweetheart. We'll find a place and get your nail fixed right after the interview. Try not to use your finger."

After taking a deep breath, Lola smiled. "I'm ready."

It looked like they were ready to go. Eunice held up her phone. "Someone call me."

Gus pulled out his phone and punched in her number. Eunice's phone burbled. "Agent 99, reporting for duty."

Chapter Twenty-One

I T WAS AN ordinary neighborhood—a little shabby, but nothing dark or nefarious. Eunice inhaled deeply and slid the phone with the open line carefully into her pocket, then opened the car door. "Herman, release the trunk. I'll get out the walker. That way you men won't attract any attention."

Eunice scampered out of the car and retrieved Lola's walker. In no time, the two of them were walking up the sidewalk to Jonas Hogg's house. She glanced at the artificial tulips, which were the same as those in front of Robert's house. It would be interesting to see if there was any more evidence of Loretta here."

"Shouldn't be anything left if the two of them are divorced."

Normally, Eunice would agree, but about half the time only one person wanted a divorce while the other one would be content to go on with things the way they were. That was certainly her case, except her husband would have been the one to keep things the way they had been. "Depends. I guess we'll find out soon. Someone just moved the curtains. He must know we're here."

The green front door with a faux wood WELCOME sign opened slowly. Outlined by the door frame was a slightly built man with a receding hairline and coke bottle glasses. Eunice nodded her head in greeting while cataloging everything he was wearing. He could almost be Robert's twin from his short sleeve dress shirt to his baggy khakis. Too bad Jake wasn't here. He might be able to tell her if the man was an actual nerd or just a hipster pretending to be.

"Welcome." The man pushed open the screen door. "Come in. I assume one of you is Lola, and you're not here to invite me to Wednesday night Bible study."

He laughed hard at his own joke, spitting a little as he did so. Eunice stepped back while Lola raised her eyebrows, then smiled. "No, I'm Lola. This is my assistant, Eunice. We're here in hopes of finding out more about Loretta and possibly locating her."

Jonas pushed up his slipping glasses, then gestured to the living room. "Can you make it okay over the lip of the doorway?"

"I'm fine," Lola declared and lifted the walker to enter the room. "I mainly use this for balance. That's all."

A club chair, a sofa, and a rocker occupied the living room. Stretched between the furniture was a floral rug. Multi-level end tables bookended the sofa. Delicate glass animals crowded one table. Photographs crowded the other. It looked like the couple in the photos were Loretta and Jonas. They were mugging at the camera, proving that they were happy once.

Eunice took the rocker and realized she was too far away to pick up voices very well on her phone. Since Lola took the club chair, she could hardly dump the woman out of it. Sitting on the sofa with Jonas would be a bit peculiar. Instead, she picked up the rocker and moved it close to the sofa. She explained by pointing to her ear.

Jonas nodded. "I understand. I think it's great you ladies are still working. I'm not sure what you expect to do that the police haven't done already."

"Did the police come and talk to you?" Eunice asked. A quick cut of the eyes from Lola made her remember her job was to be quiet and allow Lola to conduct the interview.

Jonas exhaled audibly before speaking. "Not at first. After a while, one detective came by. Not sure what I could tell him since I hadn't seen her in a month or more."

A month? She caught that. Did Lola catch that? It was hard to tell since Lola was staring at her nail. "Ah, Jonas. Loretta remarried. Why did she come by to see you?"

"Not me." His face dropped, and he looked as mournful as a basset hound. "She came by to see Cutie Pie. He's our baby."

At the word *baby*, Lola jerked, possibly remembering her role in this whole scenario. "You and Loretta have a child?"

"Not exactly," Jonas replied and pushed up from the couch. "I'll be right back."

Lola glanced at Eunice who shrugged her shoulders. It might be a good time to get the pepper spray ready just in case he returned with a weapon. Although the spray would be of little use against a gun. From her pocket, a tinny voice asked, "What's going on?"

"Shush!" was all Eunice could say before Jonas walked backed into the room, cuddling a small animal of some kind.

"Here's our sugar." Jonas lifted one of his hands, revealing a tiny white head and bright, intelligent eyes. A long tail hung beneath his hand. It had to be a mouse on steroids or a…

"Rat!" squeaked Lola. Her face flushed as she reached for her walker, readying herself if she needed to leave in a hurry.

It looked like Eunice was going to have to handle the question and answer portion of the program. Jonas held the rat out for Eunice to pet. She ran one finger over the soft coat to appease the man, but Lola refused to do even that. Instead, she leaned back as far she could to put distance between her and the rodent.

Eunice cleared her throat, then said, "You mentioned Loretta used to come over and visit Cutie Pie?"

"Oh yeah. When we first got divorced, she moved in with one of her friends at the salon. The woman had five cats. Needless to say, it was a hostile environment for any rat." He gave a little sniff. "It's not like I wanted to give her up. Cutie Pie was all I had left of Loretta. It was our only tie. I kept hoping that maybe she'd come back to me." He curled one hand to hold the rat against his chest and reached for the photo and handed it to Eunice. "Look at how happy we were."

"You two do look happy. What changed?" Eunice knew it might not be the most delicate question, but she didn't have all day. Lola was ready to bolt, and Gus might say something in the car, which would be broadcasted from her pocket.

His eyes took on a sheen as he looked away and swallowed hard. "I ask myself that every day. Loretta's really good at nails. All kinds of women came to see her. Usually, those who had exciting lives. They'd chatter about all the places they'd visited, things they'd done, and the various men they had gone through. When she'd tell me the tales she'd heard at work, I could see a faraway look in her eyes."

Jonas breathed in deeply as if to stop himself from crying. "Then, suddenly, it was wham, bam, I want a divorce, and she was gone. We had been high school sweethearts. She asked me to the Sadie Hawkins dance when we were fifteen. Neither one of us ever had eyes for another. Hanging around all those fast lane women made her think she was missing out on something. I didn't fight the divorce. We got one of those online things and filed it at the courthouse. The whole time I thought it was a bad dream I would wake from."

The emotions pouring from Jonas got to Eunice. For Pete's sake, she almost felt like she was going to cry. Did she even have any tissues in her purse? Since her hand was already wrapped around the pepper spray, she didn't dare move it. Right now, she needed another question to prompt Jonas. Across from her, Lola had pushed herself back into the club chair and had her gaze riveted on the white rat. No help there.

"Ah, where did Loretta meet her new husband or do you know?"

A low growl erupted from Jonas, then he blinked, before resuming his slightly sorrowful countenance. "Sorry. Just thinking of that piece of garbage makes my blood boil." He took a moment to collect himself and started again. "Loretta won a trip to Vegas for selling a lot of nail products. A couple of her wilder friends went along, and I'm not sure what happened. All I know is she met Robert." He spat the name. "They had a quickie wedding. Weird. I wondered if someone gave her some drugs out in Vegas, and it messed with her head. After the wedding, I didn't see her for a while, and Cutie Pie was so depressed."

No need to mention that he had to have been depressed, too. It seemed like a good time for a question to break the mood, but Eunice had nothing. Lola piped up. "You said she was a nail tech?"

"The best," he confirmed with a head bob.

"That must mean she worked in a salon close to here?"

Eunice could see where she was going with this. It wasn't exactly what they needed, but it might help.

"Glamour Nails. It was in the strip mall by the grocery store."

Lola perked up. "I think we passed it."

"It's not there anymore. The nail business is brutal. There's always someone opening a new store a block away, offering a dollar off a manicure or free nail art on a pedicure. Most customers are finicky and will shop around. Lore, my pet name for her, had regular customers who were faithful to her. Once she left, they did."

"Makes sense," Eunice added, not feeling like she had to say much. It felt like the man was just waiting for some sympathetic soul to unburden himself.

"It was a dark time when she left. I couldn't eat or sleep." He placed the rat on the couch beside him and shot it a fond gaze. He left it there and started talking again. "I didn't think I was going to make it. I even decided to get her name tattooed on my arm to show she was always in my heart."

"Did you?"

"I tried. The guy at the tattoo place talked me out of it. Told me it would be off-putting to other women when I started dating again."

"Sounds about right. Did you and Loretta ever fight?" Eunice was thinking about the loud arguments that Robert's neighbors reported.

"No." He cocked his head, blinked, then straightened it. "We loved all the same things. Same food, music, movies, you name it. That's why the divorce was so hard. I understand why she had to do it." He said the last words as if he had just figured it out.

"Why?" Loretta's behavior had baffled everyone thus far.

"Excitement, of course. She wasn't getting any younger and needed to see what she was missing."

It didn't ring true. Cutie Pie, possibly attracted by Lola's glittery nails, moved slowly closer to her, then hopped onto the club chair arm. Lola screeched, shot up, grabbed her walker, and headed for the door.

"You're scaring Cutie Pie!" Jonas declared as he hurried to catch his rat before it went out the door with her.

Inside Eunice's pocket, voices started yelling. "What's happening? Do you need help?"

At Jonas's bewildered look, "Podcast," Eunice explained with a weak smile. "I had it on pause. I was going to listen to it later. It's been great talking to you." She patted the man on the shoulder. "Things will get better," she promised, then turned to hurry after Lola.

Herman was at the trunk stowing the walker while both Jake and Gus had started up the sidewalk with determined expressions and fisted hands, as if that was going to do any good. Her pepper spray would have served the purpose better.

She held one hand up like a traffic cop. "Stop. Everything's okay. I'll explain in the car."

Once the car was in motion and everyone had calmed down, Lola exclaimed, "We forgot to pay him!"

"Good," Herman said and grinned. "It'll be one of the few times I actually got money back. The day keeps getting better and better."

Jake, who had been half-turned watching the rear windshield, spoke in a low, serious timber. "Don't start celebrating yet. We're being followed."

At times, Jake could be a bit of an alarmist. He sometimes saw things that weren't there.

Sometimes, people accused her of doing the same, but most of the time she was right. "Are you sure?"

"Definitely. It was the same car that followed us from the center. What's the likelihood they would be going to the same place?"

It wasn't likely. In the movies, the driver would erupt into a high-speed car chase, turning corners on two wheels and cutting through alleys. Not really doable with Herman driving. Eunice sucked in her lips, trying to tamp down her rising apprehension. She should have known something like this would happen when she heard the dog howl. It was an omen. "What should we do?"

Jake turned back to address the group. "There are two men in the car. They know I spotted them. We need to get to a brightly lit, crowded public venue. They won't do anything there. Also, someone needs to call Lance."

Of all the times to have a crisis, Eunice thought as she squeezed her eyes shut. She was so close to getting visiting rights with her own cat.

Chapter Twenty-Two

THE SENIOR SLEUTHS held their breath as Herman floored the car and careened around the corner without signaling. A few hard turns followed, having them weaving back and forth as if on a carnival ride. There was a rumble of thunder, then a flash of lightning followed by the onslaught of rain. It came down so fast that it made it almost impossible for the windshield wipers to keep up.

"I can't see where I'm going."

"Watch for the headlights, sweetie," Lola reassured her nervous beau. "If you can't see, they can't see."

Jake had turned to watch the pursuing car's progress. It was too late to be circumspect about being seen. "*They* don't need to see where they are going. All they have to do is follow your taillights."

"Thanks for the helpful advice," Herman grumbled, as he swerved to avoid something.

Why didn't they see the obvious? Eunice pounded on the back of the driver's seat. "Turn off your lights! Change lanes. Turn into a neighborhood. Make use of your car being gray! They're the hardest to see in weather conditions like these."

"But," Herman protested, "the other drivers won't see me."

"You'll see them," she pointed out.

"I think it's illegal."

Lola held up her phone. "I got Lance on the line. We can ask him."

That would give the bad guys plenty of time to catch up with them. Eunice gave the seat another slap. "Do it."

To her surprise, Herman did turn out the lights, switched lanes, and made a turn at a gas station. He then sped through the neighborhood and soon found himself making endless turns into a neighborhood that was equivalent to a rabbit warren. Unfortunately, the sudden storm had triggered the street lights.

Lola recounted the events to Lance, then answered with a series of *yeses* and *nos*. Finally, she said, "I'm putting you on speakerphone."

Lance's voice was a little hard to hear with the storm raging outside. "Are you sure you're being followed?"

"Yes!" Jake, Eunice, and Gus shouted. Lola may have deferred because she was holding the phone and didn't want to blast out the detective's eardrums.

"I think we lost them," Herman confidently reported. "Due to my superior driving skills."

The sound of Lance's voice filled the interior of the car. "Why are they following you?"

"That's a good question," Eunice said. "Jake didn't mention it until we were leaving Loretta's ex's house.

Instead of Lance's voice, it was the very recognizable voice of Marci. "You what?"

Lance needlessly added, "Marci is here, too."

It appeared as if the romance between the two was still progressing. "I told you that you were off the case. No case. Comprende?"

Apparently, romance didn't make her into a kinder, gentler person. No one chose to answer the question as Herman made yet another turn into a street that looped into another street. Aggravated, he sighed heavily and turned on the headlights, possibly assuming that the danger was over.

"Where are you?" Lance asked.

"Clarksville," Eunice offered. "We seem to be in one of those new neighborhoods where every house looks pretty much like the last one. There must be hundreds of them. Herman keeps trying to find a way out. We're trying to get to a well-lit public place with lots of people."

"Good plan. Keep the phone on, Lola. Someone else needs to use their phone for GPS. Punch in the words *shopping center* and go to the closest one. Make sure to tell me which one. I'll have the police waiting. Are you really sure someone was following you?"

Herman passed his phone back, which was surprising since he was protective of his phone with all its bells and whistles. "Use my phone. The passcode is 0000."

Gus grabbed it before Eunice could and immediately started searching for shopping centers. "There's one about a mile away. Northern Woods. It has a grocery and a bunch of little shops. I've punched the directions link."

A sultry voice came from Herman's phone. *"Take a sharp left, honey, in two hundred feet."*

"Who's that?" Lola inquired.

"It's a joke," Herman rushed to explain. "Possibly courtesy of the two jokers in the back seat."

Instead of defending himself, Jake cleared his throat. "Might want to turn off those headlights. They're back."

"Who?" Lance demanded.

"Our buddies who can't seem to stay away," Lola answered.

"Describe the car," Lance inquired.

The sultry voice purred, "*Another turn coming up, my hunk of burning love. It's on the left. Almost there.*"

Jake was up on his knees peering through the back window. "Navy or black sedan. It looks like a late model. I think it's a Chevrolet, but not sure. It's hard to tell in this weather. They have those expensive blue headlights. It's hard to see much more. Two men. Passenger is rolling down the window. Sticking something out the window. It's a gun! Duck!"

There was a high whine, then a thud. The back window cobwebbed. Herman swerved and moaned. The rest of the sleuths huddled out of range and were silent. Only the phones were speaking.

"*Turn right in fifty feet, sweetie.*"

"Was that a shot?" Marci asked. "Do something, Lance!"

"Keep moving," Lance instructed. "I need to know what street you're on. Look at the phone. Don't put your head up."

"Evergreen Boulevard," Gus answered back.

"Good. Now, I need you all to listen closely. Drive to the grocery. Drive up on the sidewalk if you have to. Get out of the car and into the store fast. Once inside, hide. Help Lola because there'll be no time for a walker. Do you understand?"

"Yes," they all murmured together.

The well-lit central street beckoned as Herman turned onto it and floored the gas pedal once again. Even from her crouched position, Eunice could feel the increased speed. "You're going to get pulled over."

"That's my plan," Herman pushed out the words behind clenched teeth.

Good one! Eunice was only sorry she hadn't thought of it first. The increased illumination indicated they were close to the shopping center. The GPS confirmed it with, "*Your destination is on the right, hot stuff.*"

"Get ready!" Herman announced. "I'm going to pull up on the sidewalk." Seat belts were loosened as the sleuths tensed their muscles, ready to run like they hadn't run in the last thirty years.

The front wheels bumped up onto the sidewalk as the car screeched to a stop. "Go! Go!" Herman yelled as he flung himself out of the car and raced for the passenger side where Lola was already pushing out. The scream of sirens sounded behind them as they ran into the brightly lit store, attracting the attention of the shoppers inside.

Gus warned those who were about to exit the store. "You don't want to go out there right now."

The sound of gunfire had some of the patrons looking for cover, while the not-so-wise-ones crowded the windows for a clearer view. A bullhorn was brought out after a few minutes. "*You're surrounded. You're not going anywhere. Come out with your hands up, now!*"

Even though she knew it wasn't the best thing to do, Eunice crept forward, ducking under one man's outstretched arm to catch a glimpse of the baddies. It would be good to know who was trying to put the sleuths out of business. Two thirty-ish fellows with good haircuts and mainly dressed in black were being cuffed by the police.

She had never seen the two before. Herman and Lola joined her at the window.

Herman shook his head. "Why were they chasing us? Have either one of you seen them before?"

A head shake served as Eunice's answer, but Lola waited a little longer to reply. "I don't know them but know the type. Low-level thugs on someone's payroll. You can tell by the clothes and the haircuts they're being paid well. I'd say organized crime."

Despite their sprint into the grocery store, Lola still held the phone. Marci and Lance kept asking what was happening and told the sleuths to stay inside until they got there.

"Another case solved," Herman announced.

"Not hardly." Eunice wasn't sure how he missed the obvious. "No Loretta. No clue why those guys were shooting at us. Technically, we were off the case, too."

Jake joined them at the window. "Sounds to me like our Little Mary Sunshine is back to normal."

It may have been meant as a dig, but Eunice held on to the word *our*. It meant she was actually part of the group as opposed to someone they had grudgingly admitted to keep her quiet. Call it a little triumph, but it was still a triumph, all the same.

Chapter Twenty-Three

THE GROCERY MANAGER was kind enough to allow the police to use his office to take statements from the sleuths. Another uniformed officer moved Herman's car since Lance insisted, they couldn't leave until he and Marci arrived.

From the questions they asked, it was clear that the officers considered them a bunch of bored seniors that may have heard something on the news and decided to play private eye. Eunice yearned to point out the cold cases they had solved, but she didn't. No use getting Marci and Lance in trouble. Most folks were of the opinion that old folks seldom did more than watch television and complain about various aches and pains.

When questioned, she smiled up at the young officer and placed a hand over her heart. "Oh, my, you *are* handsome. You could be a movie star. I'd say you're the spitting image of Tab Hunter."

"Who?" the young officer asked with a furrowed brow.

Kids nowadays. So unaware of the classic movie stars. She cocked her head to one side. "I think you're even more handsome than Tab. You have that clean-cut look along with just a trace of mischief. Rather like Clark Gable."

Another officer motioned to the younger officer to hurry up. The Tab Hunter twin flashed her a smile and asked, "Were you being shot at?"

"We were. I imagine there are still some bullets in Herman's car."

He wrote something on his tablet with a stylus, then looked up. "Do you know the reason for the shooting?"

Eunice batted her eyelashes. "I was hoping you'd find that out. After all, you're one of the good guys."

His eyes twinkled as he replied, "I promise to do my best."

"That's all anyone can ask for," Eunice answered and stood. She hurried to where the other sleuths were standing. Gus grumbled just low enough for her to hear. "I saw you flirting with that cop."

"True. It was part of my routine. By now you should realize the younger ones have stereotypes for the elderly. I just play into them. Sometimes, it makes life easier and helps avoid being asked the hard questions. I don't want to lie to the law."

After the police finished questioning the five, there was not much left to do, especially since Herman's car was being towed for evidence.

"I'm hungry," Gus announced. "Let's hit the deli."

About twenty minutes later, Marci and Lance found them in the tiny dining room section of the deli, chowing down on fried chicken and potato salad. Marci insisted on hugging every sleuth extra tight. Lance got down to the business of debriefing them.

"As you know, I took you off the case." He turned his head to Marci. "Didn't I take them off the case?"

"You did," she answered and made a point of making eye contact with each sleuth. "Do you know why you were off the case?"

"Open case?" Eunice guessed. At least, that's what they had been told.

"Yes, it's still an open case. That much is true, but there have been rumors about organized crime moving into the aɩea.

Wait. This was something she hadn't heard about. It made sense as to why they didn't want the sleuths involved. "Why didn't you tell us *that*?"

Marci arched her eyebrows. "Would it have made any difference?

"Yes."

"No."

"Maybe."

"Depends."

"What she said."

It was hard to know who said what, but she could see Marci's point. "Did you tell Jake to say Loretta was dead?"

"Absolutely not," Marci said. She pointed to Lance. "He did."

Instead of glaring at Lance, Eunice joined Lola and Herman in glowering at Jake.

An incensed Gus scooted away from Jake. "I defended you. I even fought to bring you in on the case."

"I appreciate it, too—" Jake began, but Lance interrupted.

"Gentlemen, we need to get you back to the center. We only brought one vehicle so we'll have to take you in shifts. Marci, what will you do if I take the men home first?"

Lola held up her hand. "There's a nail salon next door. I really do have a nail emergency."

Did she hear the woman right? "When we were running for our lives you noticed there was a nail salon next door?"

"Of course not. I saw it when the police were cuffing the thugs. It's hard to miss a glowing neon hand with painted nails."

Eunice hadn't noticed it. She blinked twice and glared at the sign as if it were at fault for her lack of observation. It would serve her well to step up her game.

They could call an Uber, but it would be fairly expensive to drive to the next city. Besides, she could keep Lola company and discover what all this salon business was about. They said goodbye to the guys and made a slow parade with Lola's walker and Marci's cane to the salon next door.

Without realizing how it happened, Eunice found herself sitting in a massage chair talking to a woman who had to be Loretta's twin, except her hair was bleached blonde. Her mouth twisted to one side as she considered the likelihood of two women who resembled each other living in the same area and having the exact same profession had to be astronomical. It had to be Loretta. To test her theory, Eunice poured out the details of her day.

The woman wore a name tag with *Sally* emblazoned on it. As she buffed away the calluses, Sally asked, "You mean to tell me that man with the rat is still in love with his wife?"

"Definitely," Eunice replied. "It was touching to see someone that much in love. It was hard to believe it wasn't returned at least a little.

"After everything his ex did, he still cares." Sally murmured the statement, appearing thoughtful as she massaged a citrus-scented scrub onto Eunice's feet and legs.

Eunice continued, "He believes she must have had a reason. Said something about her wanting to have a more exciting life."

"Hmm... Chasing after excitement is the best way to get bit in the butt. Sounds like a stupid woman to me," Sally commented, as she cupped the warm water and washed off the scrub.

The tap-tap of Marci's cane signaled her approach. She boosted herself into the chair next to Eunice's and winked at the sleuth before addressing her, "Telling her about your day?"

"I sure was," Eunice answered.

Marci eased back into the massage chair and turned it on. "It would be wonderful if we could get someone to testify against the monster who sent those men after you and your senior friends."

"What would happen to the person who testified?"

"I imagine a deal could be worked out. They could even be put in the witness protection program." Marci played with the controls on the chair and upped the massage tension until she was shaking from the roller bars. After a few seconds, she dialed it back down.

Eunice gave Sally a speculative look, wondering what it would take to reach her. "That wouldn't be such a bad thing, would it, *Loretta*?"

Loretta stopped in the process of drying Eunice's feet. Her shoulders slumped, and she sighed heavily. "I'm so tired of running and hiding," she murmured, trying to hold back visible tears.

Marci stopped fiddling with the chair controls and alternated her gaze between a glassy-eyed nail tech and a rather smug Eunice.

Loretta picked up the towel she'd just dried Eunice's feet with and wiped her nose with it. "Who should I talk to?"

"I'm your girl," Marci placed a hand on her chest. "I'm temporarily on medical leave, but I can go with you."

"Would you?" A tear finally slid down the woman's face. "This has been such a long nightmare. At first, I thought Antonio was charming. I don't know if that's his real name, but that's the one he used in Vegas. He was so attentive. He even begged me to stay after the other nail techs flew home. Before I knew it, I was tying the knot with a man I barely knew. I had no clue he was a criminal. When I found out, he told me I would be charged as an accessory.

"We fought all the time about it. He invented this fake life here with his new *Robert* persona since many big-time dealers find it's much easier working out of small cities or towns and looking ordinary. We were anything *but* ordinary."

By then, Loretta was crying hard, attracting the attention of other customers.

Lola wandered near, waving her newly repaired nail while exclaiming, "It has to be a man to cause that sort of heartache."

Because of the situation, Marci called in extra security. When Lance arrived, Marci briefed him quickly and promised to see him later. The ladies climbed into the car while Marci and Loretta left in a squad car.

Lola put out her hand in the meager sunlight that had shown up after the storm. "My nail is as good as new. Without my broken nail, we would never have solved the case."

It was hard to admit the woman was right. "I guess we should all be grateful for acrylic nails. Too bad Loretta broke down before she painted my toenails."

"No worries," Lola informed her. "I'll let you have my next appointment."

Wow. Eunice mouthed the word. First, Jake referred to her as Our Mary Sunshine and now Lola was giving up a nail appointment. Maybe she really *did* have friends after all.

Epilogue

L IGHT STREAMED OUT of the pole barn, especially from the two front doors thrown wide. A fiddler warming up picked out the first notes of "Turkey in the Straw." Greener Pastures residents arrived via electric golf carts. Most were decked out in cat ears, pajamas, or even pajamas with cats on them. They greeted the Square Dance Committee consisting of Carmen, Pearl, and Eunice. The trio stood by the open door, welcoming all the participants.

Debbi, the dance instructor, showed up in regular dance attire sporting cat ears and had drawn on whiskers and a cute black nose. Bob had a snap button western-style shirt with kittens all over it. They greeted everyone with smiles, but Debbi took hold of Eunice's hands. "This is so amazing. I would never have thought of hosting a Cat's Pajamas Dance."

On any other day, Eunice would enjoy being in the spotlight, but tonight it embarrassed her to be singled out. "It was nothing. Some of the residents were concerned about not having the proper attire. I had noticed from my stay here most loved cats and many have pajamas. It seemed like a sure thing. Also, it was a way to celebrate Domino."

Pearl, who stood beside Eunice, corrected her. "Chairman Me-ow."

Instead of replying to the remark, Eunice kept on talking, not even upset with Pearl. "Domino was such a special cat who was with us for such a brief time."

"Oh." Debbi patted Eunice's hand. "I'm so sorry. Did he die?"

"No, nothing like that. We're not allowed to have personal pets at the center. I'm sure the place would become a zoo in no time if we could. I'm not sure if you remember Marci, our recovering detective? She finally got to go home, and she took Domino with her."

"Chairman Meow," Pearl added, despite no one paying a lick of attention to her.

Eunice almost felt sorry for the woman. So bossy and everything had to be her way. It was ironic that Carmen was the one who turned her in for having a cat. Thankfully, Marci had already made plans to relocate and volunteered to adopt the cat with the promise of the two of them coming back for return visits.

Debbi gave her hand a final pat. "I'm so glad things worked out." She nodded to Pearl and Carmen. "I'll see you on the dance floor."

Apparently, that wasn't enough for Pearl, who elbowed Carmen. "She didn't even call us by name."

"She probably doesn't know them," Carmen added matter-of-factly as she acknowledged the happy residents leaving their staff-driven golf carts.

The smell of barbecue wafted through the air as the kitchen staff arrived with foil-covered pans. Eunice knew most of the staff by name and called out to them. "Appreciate your help, Wade! Thanks for staying late, Janice."

"No problem," Wade replied, his biceps straining as he carried in the heavy pans.

A grinning cook unloaded a large white box and carried it cautiously to Eunice. "Peek inside. I think you'll be surprised."

Inside the box were cupcakes and each one was decorated with a cat face. "Wonderful! So clever, too."

Carmen floated after the cook, possibly interested in the cupcakes or just tired of listening to Pearl gripe about everything. Eunice felt obliged to stay and welcome everyone. Lance and Marci were next. Even though Marci wasn't up to dancing, she still made an appearance. Lance would sit by her and keep up a running commentary. Marci would let him. They were so perfect for each other.

Marci hugged Eunice and whispered, "I'll round up the other sleuths and give a brief recap of what's happening with Robert and his thugs."

Lance hugged her, and they both proceeded into the pole barn. Pearl watched them go with a dismissive sniff. "They didn't even talk to me."

"They don't know you," Eunice lied. She had told them all about the catnapping Pearl and all the hoops she made Eunice jump through to visit with her own cat. While Eunice had no real proof of the woman's perfidy, she suspected. "I *could* introduce you."

"You should have when they came in," Pearl pointed out in an accusatory tone.

Even though most of the guests were inside dancing, Eunice insisted on waiting outside. She gestured to the dancers forming squares. "You can go in."

"I just might. Oh look, it's that trashy former showgirl and Herman." Pearl wrinkled her nose as if smelling something foul.

To be fair, Eunice had been tolerant all night. Besides, she was new at being kind. Her nostrils flared as she tried to hold back her anger and pointed to the interior of the barn. "You need to go, now. Don't ever let me hear you talk about my friend in that manner again."

Pearl slunk inside, casting a bewildered glance over her shoulder. Eunice shook her head. The woman had no clue. Had she, Eunice, really been that bad? Surely not. She may have been a trifle abrupt, but never that bad.

Herman and Lola stopped to greet Eunice with a warm greeting and a hug. Lola indicated the departing Pearl. "I see you routed the witch."

"Please…" Eunice began, "you really shouldn't talk about witches that way." They all chuckled.

Herman gestured to the barn. "How did you score this?"

"Eavesdropping." It was one of her premier skills. "I knew the pole barn was done. They were going to purchase some snow removal and lawn equipment to put into it. It would save on hiring a lawn service and snow removal companies. I took a chance and asked the head administrator if we could please use it for a dance for the residents."

"He said yes just like that?" Herman waggled his shaggy brows.

"He had to. I asked him while he was showing around possible new residents. He couldn't afford to look like a crab when he hoped to impress the potentials with what a great place Greener Pastures is."

"Oh my!" Herman chuckled and slapped Eunice on the back, causing her to stumble a wee bit. "I'm certainly glad we have you on the sleuths' side."

With Marci back at home and back to work soon, Eunice wondered what would happen to the sleuths. "Do you think there will be any more cold cases?"

Lola winked. "You know it. Just wait and see. We have a four for four record. Not sure how it will happen but it will. I'm putting my money on the Senior Sleuths continuing."

"I hope so." Eunice really did. It was the first place she felt like she belonged. "Marci and Lance are already inside and waiting for the gang to gather and hear the rundown on New Albany's crime wave."

"I want to hear that…" Herman replied. Lola nudged Eunice. "Lookee who's coming and he has a rose for you-know-who. We'll catch up with you two later. They waved at Gus, then turned away to give them some privacy.

Gus had cleaned up pretty well. He didn't own any cat decorated pajamas or shirts. He had a photo of Domino made into a large button that he had pinned to his shirt pocket. "Hey, beautiful. You've been saving all your dances for me?"

He offered the rose, which Eunice accepted. She fingered the velvety petals. "Not sure if you want to dance with me. I'm not that good. I missed more classes than I attended. Obviously, I'm not a great square dancer like your late wife, Maureen."

"No, you're not Maureen, but I don't want you to *be* Maureen. She was a part of my life, but that part's over. I need you to be Eunice. You need to tell me when I mess up. As for dancing, square dancing is supposed to be fun, not a competition. Maureen never could remember that. Let's go have some fun. Ever since I met you my life has been filled with fun and excitement."

That was so sweet. It made her sigh a little. Some of the excitement came from the cold cases, but she'd still take credit. She leaned over and kissed Gus on the cheek. "Let's go kick up our heels, but first we need to be debriefed on Loretta's situation and *Robert*." She managed to enunciate the last name with a sneer. It was no secret how Eunice felt about him.

She tucked her hand into Gus's bent arm and carried her rose in her free hand, garnering some envious glances from a few of the female residents. They weaved through the red and blue checked tablecloths. Each one had a mason jar with a tiny flickering LCD candle inside. Pearl should be pleased, but probably wasn't.

At a table farthest away from the dancing and the music sat Lance and Marci. They were already joined by Herman and Lola. There was a break in the music and the four attempted to wave Jake over, but he was commandeered by a woman who needed a partner before he could make it to the table.

Gus pulled out a chair for Eunice when they reached the table, and they sat. The music had started again, and the squares with four couples in each had assembled and were ready to go. A red-faced Jake mouthed something in their direction, but no one could hear or understand him.

Eunice wrinkled her nose. It was obvious when men were in short supply, and Jake was a willing dancer—nothing short of being carted away in a gurney would excuse him from a dance.

"You know the man is going to dance all night. He'll complain about it tomorrow, too, about his feet hurting and how tired he is. He's loving it, though. Tell us what you're going to tell us, and we'll relate it to Jake later."

Lance pondered the suggestion, but Marci moved on it. "Okay, lean in." She motioned the sleuths closer. All of them scooted their chairs closer as if they were about to share a secret, which they were. No one had a clue one of the city's best crime units was sitting in their midst.

"It wasn't too hard to nail *Robert*," Marci confided. "His baby thugs had no loyalty whatsoever. They even explained what they knew about his drug distribution and number rackets. Fortunately, the information Loretta gathered is much more extensive.

"As for the thugs, they aren't the sharpest knives in the drawer. I know you thought you were clever with the mail delivery con. Robert saw through that and assumed you'd lead him to Loretta, which is why he hired Dumb and Dumber."

"Would he have killed her?" Lola gasped the question and put her hands up to her cheeks.

Marci inhaled deeply, grimaced, and rubbed both palms over her face. "It's possible. That's what bad guys do. They aren't big fans of talking out issues."

This caused murmuring around the table—mostly concern for Loretta, but gratitude they had survived. Herman cleared his throat. "Do you think I'll get my car back soon? Better yet, do you think insurance will honor the repairs? I don't recall any coverage for being shot at on the policy."

Lance fielded that question. "You can have your car back, but it might serve you better if we just tow it to the body shop."

"That would work," Herman agreed.

Gus held up one finger, then cupped his hand around his ear as he spoke. "I know my hearing is somewhat impaired. I thought you said the shooters were following us to find Loretta."

"In a way," Marci agreed with a head bob. "Actually, their intentions were to scare you into not investigating Robert. When questioned, they said they only meant to stop and talk to you."

"Shooting doesn't usually make people stop," Eunice pointed out.

"They were actually going for the tires," Marci said and arched her eyebrows. "I must say, Herman, you were quite the driver that they didn't catch you or damage your tires, either."

The flattery made the man chuckle and beam. That was well and good, but Eunice wanted to know about Loretta. "What happened to our favorite nail tech?"

Marci and Lance exchanged glances, then Lance spoke. "For the record, we can't really say anything. She and her family are currently in a safe house. Once she testifies, Loretta and her family will be under the witness protection agency. We can assume wherever they go they will be fine.

Eunice knew Jonas, Loretta, and Cutie Pie would be very appreciative of their new beginning. There was no mention of what Eunice really wanted to know. "When are you bringing Domino for a visit?"

Laughter greeted her question. "What's so funny?" Eunice demanded.

There was a rustle as wallets were opened and five-dollar bills were pulled out and passed over to Gus. Her sweetie winked at her. "We bet on how long it would be before you mentioned Domino. I told them you were much more patient than before. You lasted ten minutes, which made me the winner."

Eunice placed her hand on the money. "*I'm* the winner, in more ways than one. That's my money. If you play your cards right, I might buy you a soda."

The End

Sailor Take Warning

Book Eleven in The Painted Lady Inn Mysteries

Available May 2020

THE ROUND GOLDEN sun glistened in the pristine blue skies rather like a Christmas ornament, except it was May. The low hum of the waves punctuated with an occasional childish scream of joy as a child met the ocean for the first time provided background sound. Donna Tollhouse, innkeeper, and her sister-in-law Maria stood on The Painted Lady Inn's wraparound porch while peering in the direction of the ocean, which would have been visible if the trees hadn't leafed out so much.

"I could help with your regatta-themed dishes," Maria offered with a grin.

There were a few more screams, not so childish but equally playful. Donna, who had been holding Baby Cici, her niece, cut her eyes to her sister-in-law Maria and asked, "Did they hire another half dozen hot lifeguards this year?"

"Oh my!" Maria rolled her eyes and waved her hand in front of her face as if the thought heated her up. "You should see them. I doubt they'll be here long. Most probably have aspirations to be models or actors."

"Well then," Donna began, then cast a mischievous glance behind her where her husband Mark was seated in one of the wicker chairs reading the local newspaper. "It's been quite a while since I've taken a stroll on the beach."

Mark lowered his newspaper to reply, "I'll be more than glad to take a walk on the beach with you. No reason for you to join the mob of Legacy women drooling over boys young enough to be your son."

A derisive snort erupted from Maria. "There's a female lifeguard, or maybe two, attracting all the old geezers' attention."

Leave it to Maria to go for the zinger. Even though she knew her husband was teasing about the lifeguards being young enough to be her son, the fact it could be true nettled her some. Sure, she'd never see fifty again. Since she married late, she'd never have children, either. The fact weighed on her as she played with her niece. Getting married and having children always seemed like one of those things she had plenty of time left to do. Until she didn't. She consoled herself with the thought she wouldn't have been a good mother since she tended to be exacting.

Baby Cici took that moment to yank on the chain holding Donna's readers. The beaded chain broke sending beads pinging and spinning across the porch. Her glasses had the good fortune to fall inside her shirt.

Maria held her hands out to take the infant. "Cici! Look at what you did."

The baby laughed and cooed with pride as if destroying the chain had been her objective. At the grand age of eleven and a half months, Cici was pulling up on the furniture and making tentative steps much to the delight of her adoring fans. Unfortunately, her beginning efforts at walking were not only wiping out the various knick-knacks scattered around the inn, but had also put a rip in one curtain. Even the inn's unofficial puggle mascot, Jasper, was startled when he was inadvertently used as a stepping block helping the curious toddler reach a tabletop.

A soft thud sounded as her husband knelt beside her to help without being asked. His actions earned him an adoring look. From Donna's position on the porch floor, she swept up the errant beads into her hand considering Maria's earlier comment. Not the one to see the hot lifeguards, but the offer of assistance. "I appreciate you offering to help."

Her sister-in-law's delicate laughter that was reminiscent of wind chimes sounded. "But," Maria said and lifted her eyebrows as she shifted her child to the other hip, "I hear what you're *not* saying. Whatever I might do doesn't balance out what havoc your niece might do in the meantime."

"I didn't say that". Although, Donna may have thought it. "I didn't think Tennyson did much when he was here, but surprisingly, without him here, I'm stressed trying to get everything done." Before her sister-in-law could reply, Donna held her hand up. "I've taken care of the matter. I put an ad in the paper for help. Even got a few calls about it. One candidate sounds ideal. She's coming by soon. Of course, you're welcome to keep working on the website and other technical aspects, if you want."

The paper rattled as Mark folded it and placed it on the wicker side table. "No need to mention you're no good at that type of thing."

"You aren't, either," Donna pointed out. Her detective husband had grumbled on more than one occasion about the hardship of logging all his official activities onto the computer. On the other hand, he'd rejoiced in how easy it was to find files on his laptop from the comfort of his own home.

"I know," he grinned, not the least upset at having his lack of computer skills pointed out to him. "I'm grateful for Maria's technical know-how. But now, I'm off to use my much-vaunted police skills over at the regatta."

Having scooped up all the errant beads, Donna stood, pocketed the items into her colorful apron that featured happy dogs dancing. "Are you going to catch a murderer?"

"Bite your tongue." He stepped closer and kissed her cheek. "I'll give the con men who floated in with the regatta the eye to let them know they're being watched. I may have to remind the uniformed officers to pay attention to the crowds, not the boats or the hot lifeguards." He exhaled audibly. "Sounds like a full day's work to me, especially walking around in a suit jacket in the noonday sun."

It wasn't the first time her honey had complained about walking around in the heat. She patted his arm. "I'm not sure why you can't opt for something a little lighter. The bicycle cops get to wear shorts."

"Dignity. I need my suit jacket because it's a symbol of authority. It gives people confidence. I can't go running around in a flowered shirt and shorts like all the other yahoos."

"I suppose." Donna pursed her lips, not totally convinced the man couldn't get by with just a shirt and khakis. "What about wearing your badge on a lanyard like they do on television?"

"That's television. Besides, I don't want to announce I'm the law until I need to."

"Yeah, as the only person there wearing a sports jacket, you'll blend in alright."

Instead of replying to her sarcasm, he removed his pen and pad from his jacket, then removed the much talked about article of clothing. "Better?"

Donna made a slow circle around her husband giving him a thorough inspection. "Much. I doubt your co-workers will recognize you without the jacket."

"Ha!" Mark forced a laugh.

Maria squatted to put down the squirming baby who immediately crawled toward the red geraniums. A quick sidestep had Donna guarding the colorful blooms.

"How about the tie?" Donna asked, knowing she was pushing her husband's personal dress code.

"What about it? You bought it. It's a good one. A little more colorful than I might have chosen, though. What's wrong with it?"

"Do you need it? You'll look like a bank president who wandered onto the beach by mistake. You still have that air of one who doesn't belong here."

He grunted as he shoved his pad and pen into his pants pocket. "You'll have me rolling up my pants and taking off my shoes and socks next."

The comment had Donna glancing at his feet, which caused Mark to hold up his hand, which was either telling her goodbye or halting any more effort to change his appearance. He smirked and dropped his hand before trotting down the sidewalk, heading toward the beach path.

Maria asked. "You think he'll take off his tie before he hits the beach?"

"He will and will probably put it back on before he comes home, too." The thought made her chuckle and shake her head. "If he removed here, it would probably seem like I was asserting undue influence. It's a control thing."

"I understand. Good thing you don't have any control issues."

"Exactly." Donna pointed to Baby Cici who was trying to reach between her legs to grab a blossom. "You might want to take her to the backyard where there are fewer plants to be plucked."

Maria lifted her baby, holding her high and letting her chubby little legs dangle as she made faces at the darling. "My goodness you've changed, Donna. Before, you might have suggested a nap, playpen, or time to go home when a toddler caused this much trouble."

"True." She pressed her hand against her chest as the fact sunk in. "Those where other people's children. Not my own blood. They weren't nearly as cute and smart as Cici." She reflected for a moment. "I think we've all changed. Would you have ever seen Mark working without his jacket before?"

The suggestion made them both laugh. A low automotive hum as a car pulled into the inn driveway interrupted their amusement and caused Donna to check her watch. "It's my candidate and she's prompt. An excellent sign. I have a good feeling about this."

Printed in Great Britain
by Amazon

57982227R00102